Irving Berdine Richman, pub Iowa. Historical dept.

John Brown Among the Quakers

and other sketches

Irving Berdine Richman, pub Iowa. Historical dept.

John Brown Among the Quakers
and other sketches

ISBN/EAN: 9783337096649

Printed in Europe, USA, Canada, Australia, Japan

Cover: Foto ©Andreas Hilbeck / pixelio.de

More available books at **www.hansebooks.com**

JOHN BROWN AMONG THE QUAKERS, AND OTHER SKETCHES

BY

IRVING B. RICHMAN
CONSUL GENERAL OF THE UNITED STATES TO SWITZERLAND

DES MOINES
THE HISTORICAL DEPARTMENT OF IOWA
1894

𝕿𝖍𝖊 𝕷𝖆𝖐𝖊𝖘𝖎𝖉𝖊 𝕻𝖗𝖊𝖘𝖘

R. R. DONNELLEY & SONS CO., CHICAGO

INTRODUCTORY NOTE.

The Historical Department of Iowa was established in 1892 by vote of the Twenty-fourth General Assembly of the State. Its object is the promotion of historical collections pertaining to Iowa and the territory from which Iowa was formed. The department is placed under the supervision of a board of trustees consisting of the Governor of the State, the Judges of the Supreme Court, the Secretary of State, and the Superintendent of Public Instruction.

The historical papers published in this volume are contributions to the work of the department. Two of them—the one on John Brown and the one on Black Hawk—have been passed upon and commended as original studies: the first by Frank B. Sanborn, Esq., Brown's biographer, and the second by the late Dr. Francis Parkman.

JOHN BROWN AMONG THE
QUAKERS

JOHN BROWN AMONG THE QUAKERS.

Is THERE *room* for another article on John Brown? It would seem to be more than doubtful. His life has been written three times: by Redpath, by Webb, and by Sanborn; by Sanborn in a way most thorough and painstaking. Many papers about him and his exploits have appeared in the magazines: not less than seven in the *Atlantic Monthly*, the first in 1865 and the last in 1879; two at least in the *Century*, and several in the *North American Review*, the *Andover Review*, and *Lippincott's*. His career in Kansas has been minutely traced; his foray in Virginia has been described by his son and by persons who were his prisoners at Harper's Ferry.

But the whole of Brown's story has not yet been told, not even by Mr. Sanborn. A part of it, and that an interesting part, remains to be told. This is the part supplied by the incidents of the sojourn of John Brown in Iowa from early in August, 1857, to April 27th, 1858, and from February 10th to about

March 7th, 1859: first at Tabor in Fremont County, and afterwards, and more especially, at Springdale in Cedar County.

If one take the cars on the western bank of the Mississippi River at Davenport in Iowa and travel west on the Chicago, Rock Island and Pacific Railroad for forty miles, he will reach the town of West Liberty in Muscatine County. Then if he travel north on the Burlington, Cedar Rapids and Northern Railroad for six miles, he will reach the town of West Branch in Cedar County. Four miles due east from West Branch is the village of Springdale. But it is with West Branch that we first have to do. One day late in October, of the year 1856, there rode into the town of West Branch (not then a railway station) an elderly man, weary and travel-stained. He was mounted on a mule and led a horse. He made his way to the only tavern in the place, over the entrance to which hung the sign, "The Traveler's Rest." This tavern was kept by a genial, rosy-cheeked Quaker by the name of James Townsend. On dismounting the traveler asked his host: "Have you ever heard of John Brown of Kansas?" According to the story, Townsend, without replying, took from his vest pocket a piece of chalk and, removing Brown's hat,

marked it with a large X; he then replaced
the hat and solemnly decorated the back of
Brown's coat with two large X marks; lastly
he placed an X on the back of the mule.
Brown in this way having been admitted to
the tavern free list, Townsend said: "Friend,
put the animals in that stable and walk into
the house; thee is surely welcome." Brown
had just come from the stirring scenes of the
Kansas Territory: from the battle of Black
Jack, fought in the preceding June, and
from Ossawatomie and the Lawrence foray,
events that then were but a few weeks past;
and the suggestion has been made that in
Brown's narrative of his Kansas adventures
worthy James Townsend received a full equiv-
alent for the buckwheat cakes and "sorghum"
for which his hostelry was famous, and to which
on this occasion John Brown doubtless did ample justice. Be that as it may, it is certain that,
during Brown's short stay in West Branch,
(he was in Chicago on Oct. 25th,) he heard
of Springdale and of the strong anti-slavery
sentiment of its shrewd, thrifty, Quaker population; for henceforth this village became
one of his places of frequent resort.

Continuing his journey from Chicago,
Brown went to Ohio, where were his family,
and thence, with a stop or two in the State of

New York, to Boston, Massachusetts. Here
he first met Mr. F. B. Sanborn then just grad-
uated from Harvard, who, twenty-eight years
afterwards, became his biographer. While in
Boston, Jan. 7th, 1857, Brown was made the
agent of the Massachusetts-Kansas State
Committee to receive two hundred Sharp's
rifles, then stored at Tabor in Iowa. These
rifles had been sent West by this committee in
August, 1856, to be used for defense by the
Free State settlers. They had got as far as
Tabor, but for reasons not known to the committee, had got no farther. During his stay
in the East, Brown appeared before the Joint
Committee of the Massachusetts Legislature
appointed to investigate the Kansas situation;
spoke in the town hall at Concord where he
had Mr. Emerson as a listener; met Theodore
Parker at the delivery of one of the latter's
discourses in Music Hall, Boston; ordered
one thousand pikes from Charles Blair of
Collinsville, Connecticut,—the handles to be
six feet in length and the ferrules to be of
strong malleable iron; and last, but by no
means least, about April 1st, met Hugh
Forbes, an Italio-Anglican swordsman and
drill master, whom he hired to go to Tabor
and make ready to drill the squad of men he
purposed to assemble there on his return to

the West. For this service Forbes was to receive one hundred dollars a month; and six hundred dollars were on April 1st, 1857, handed over to him by Brown to bind the bargain and as an advance payment. Forbes had been a silk merchant at Sienna and had served with Garibaldi in 1848–49; since coming to America he had eked out a scant subsistence as a translator on the staff of the New York *Tribune* and by giving fencing lessons. On April 13th, Brown left for the West, but did not reach Tabor until early in August.

Three facts gave Tabor its importance in slavery days: its location in a free State; the intense anti-slavery sentiment of its people; and its proximity to the northern line of Kansas territory. It had been founded in 1852 by a few families from Oberlin, Ohio, almost all of them Congregationalists; and when in 1856 access to Kansas for Northern settlers, by way of St. Louis and the Missouri River, was practically denied by the Missourians, a new route through Iowa and Nebraska Territory was opened up by Dr. S. G. Howe and other Massachusetts men; and this route had Tabor and Nebraska City for its western termini. Among the parties of Free State settlers that in 1856 came west over the new

route was one led by a Col. Eldridge. They
had started without arms, (some of them from
as distant a State as Maine,) having been
promised that arms would be supplied them
at Albany, then at Buffalo, after that at Cleveland, and finally at Chicago. But, on reaching Tabor, they still were defenseless; moreover, they were about to mutiny. They were
with difficulty persuaded to go forward by
General James H. Lane who made them a
spirited speech. It doubtless was the experience of this party, or of some similar party at
about this time, that influenced the Massachusetts-Kansas State Committee to send to the
West the two hundred Sharp's rifles which
already have been mentioned. These rifles,
on their arrival in Tabor, had been stored in
the barn on the premises belonging to the
Rev. John Todd (the Congregational clergyman of the place) to await a favorable opportunity for smuggling them through Nebraska
City and over the border into Kansas. Such
an opportunity had not yet presented itself
when in August, 1857, Brown came with his
order for the arms from the Massachusetts
Committee. They were promptly given into
his charge by Todd[1] and, on August 13th,

---

[1] I had two cannon in my barn for a considerable time,
besides boxes of guns, sabres, cartridges and clothing; also

Brown wrote to Mr. Sanborn at Boston: "I find the arms and ammunition voted me by the Massachusetts State Committee nearly all here and in middling good order—some a little rusted. Have overhauled and cleaned up the worst of them."

On August 9th, Hugh Forbes arrived. When engaged he had been directed to start West as soon as possible, but he did not do so until he had spent all of the six hundred dollars which Brown had then paid him. Now that he was on the ground with the Manual of Tactics prepared by himself, entitled the Patriotic Volunteer,¹ the business of military

twenty boxes of Sharp's rifles. Captain Brown came for them and I went out with him to the barn and showed him where they were.—*Letter of Rev. John Todd, dated May 25th, 1892.*

¹ The complete title of Forbes's book is: "Manual for the Patriotic Volunteer on Active Service in Regular and Irregular War, being the Art and Science of obtaining and maintaining Liberty and Independence." The first part of the book is devoted to "popular or irregular war," and the remainder to "regular war." There is marked similarity between the methods of irregular or guerilla warfare recommended in Forbes' book and those practiced by John Brown. Indeed, it is not improbable that Brown's methods — particularly those upon which he had decided for his Virginia campaign — were to some extent derived from this book. It is known to have been Brown's intention when he left Tabor for Ashtabula, Ohio, not merely to establish a school of instruction there but also in Canada, [Letter of C. W. Moffat to F. B. Sanborn quoted at page 425 of San-

instruction was at once begun. "We are beginning to take lessons," wrote Brown to his wife and family, on August 17th, "and have, we think, a very capable teacher." At this time there seems to have been no one with Brown at Tabor except his son Owen. Lessons in the Manual were given to Brown by Forbes and both practiced target shooting. No drilling was done by Brown in public; indeed, neither he nor Forbes was much seen. They kept themselves close. But the good opinion of Forbes, which Brown had at first conceived, did not last. He proved to be an intractable, vain-glorious person; not willing to serve in the capacity of drill-master, but desirous himself of becoming the head of a movement for liberating the slaves.[1]   The

born's Life and Letters of John Brown] thus providing for the creation of a number of bands which should operate separately yet in concert. On the advisability of bands such as these, Forbes says at paragraph 30 of the Manual: "A single band, whether large or small, would have but a poor chance of success — it would be speedily surrounded; but a multiplicity of little bands, some three to ten miles distant from each other, yet in connection and communication, cannot be surrounded, especially in a chain of well wooded mountains, such as the Appenines."

[1] "He [Forbes] said further that in the course of their [Forbes' and Brown's] conversations as to the plan by which they should more effectually counteract this invasion, [that of Kansas by the Slave States] he suggested the getting up of a stampede of slaves secretly on the border of

outcome was that on November 2d, Forbes, in disgust, left Brown for the East.[1] The measure of Brown's infatuation with Forbes on first meeting him, and even for a time after he came to Tabor, is surprising. While in the East, Brown had not taken Sanborn or Parker or Gerritt Smith into his confidence as to his Virginia plan, but to Forbes he had divulged all. It is worthy of remark in passing that the first written intimation of this plan given to any one by Brown was to his wife. It is contained in the following sentence of a letter to her from Tabor, dated August 17th: "Should no disturbance occur [in Kansas], we may possibly think best to work back eastward; cannot determine yet."

The desertion of Forbes compelled Brown to abandon his project of a school of military

Kansas and Missouri which Brown disapproved, and on his part suggested an attack upon the border States with a view to induce the slaves to rise, and so keep the invaders at home to take care of themselves."—*Senator William H. Seward in his examination before Senator Mason's Committee on the John Brown Affair.*

[1] "I had the impression it [the quarrel between Forbes and Brown] was on account of want of pay; that Brown had no men to drill; that he [Forbes] went out [to Tabor] to drill some men and they had none, and that Brown did not pay him."—*Senator Henry Wilson in his examination before Senator Mason's Committee on the John Brown Affair.*

instruction for himself and such followers as
he should succeed in gathering about him at
Tabor.   Followers themselves were scarce.
He therefore decided to go to Kansas, assemble a number of the tried men of the Kansas
conflict, proceed to Ashtabula, Ohio, and
there establish a military school at which his
men could be instructed.   He also decided
that his next move against slavery would be
made somewhere in the State of Virginia.   At
Lawrence, Kansas, he enlisted John E. Cook,
whom he had first met after the battle of
Black Jack, Luke F. Parsons, who had also
been with him in Kansas in 1856, and Richard
Realf.   At Topeka he was joined by Aaron
D. Stephens, (then known as C. Whipple,)
Charles W. Moffat, and John Henrie Kagi.
With these men he went to Tabor, where in
the meantime had come William H. Leeman
and Charles Plummer Tidd, both of whom
had formerly served with him.   Toward the
last of November he and his band left Tabor
en route for Ashtabula, but not until Brown
had said to Jonas Jones (in whose care his
letters had been coming to him and in whose
house the military lessons had been given),
" Good bye, Mr. Jones, you will hear from
me.   We've had enough talk about ' bleeding
Kansas.'   I will make a bloody spot at another

point to be talked about."[1] On leaving Tabor, Brown told Cook, Realf, and Parsons that his ultimate destination was Virginia. This was not welcome news to these three of his men, and they were with difficulty prevailed upon to accompany him. But accompany him they did, and after several weeks of hard travel over the plains, the party reached Springdale—probably late in December, 1857.

Springdale, as has been stated before, is a small village in Cedar county, Iowa. Among its first residents were John H. Painter, a Quaker, who came in 1849; and Ann Coppoc, a Quakeress, and Dr. H. C. Gill, who came in 1850. During the next few years many came, almost all of them Quakers; so that when visited by Brown and his band in 1857, it was a thriving Quaker settlement. Its one street, which in fact is but a part of the public highway, is bordered on either hand by modest frame houses surrounded by spacious yards and shaded by the over-hanging branches of trees. On all sides of the village the green and undulating fields stretch away to the horizon. Within its homes the pleasant

---

[1] This remark was made in the presence of William M. Brooks, Esq., of Tabor, now President of Tabor College. *From Letter of President Brooks, dated May 30th, 1892.*

"thee" and "thy" of the Quaker constantly
are heard; and there prevails an air of
peace and serenity which is inexpressibly
soothing and comforting. Today, twenty-
eight years after the abolition of slavery, the
men of Springdale vote the Republican ticket
with very nearly the same unanimity that they
did in 1860. From this fact one may infer
something as to the political spirit of its good
people in the 50's, when to be an Abolitionist
generally was to be more or less despised.

As has been seen, it was not Brown's original intention to stop long at Springdale. It
had been his purpose to stop there merely
long enough to sell his teams and wagons,
and then to proceed by rail to Ashtabula county,
Ohio. But the panic of '57 had begun and
money was scarce. He was nearly out of
funds, and unable to raise any. Under these
circumstances, he decided to spend the winter
at the village, and to resume his journey early
in the spring. He was more than welcome,
and so were his men. To the Quakers he and
his band stood as the embodiment of the
sentiment against human slavery which that
sect so firmly held. To be sure, John Brown
and his followers were not men of peace;
they, one and all of them, had fought hard
and often in the Kansas war; but much was

pardoned to them by the Quakers because of the holiness of their object; for, while the Quaker would not concede that bloodshed ever was right, it was with extreme leniency that he chided him who had shed blood to liberate the slave.

Brown's men—Kagi, Stephens, Cook, Realf, Tidd, Parsons, Moffat, Leeman, Owen Brown, and a negro, Richard Richardson, who had been picked up at Tabor, were given quarters in the house of Mr. William Maxon which was situated about three miles northeast of the village. Maxon himself was not a Quaker, and the direct responsibility of housing men-at-arms was thus avoided by this Quaker community. Brown, however, was received into the house of the good Quaker, John H. Painter, who became one of his staunchest and most confidential friends. The time spent in Springdale was a time of genuine pleasure to Brown's men. They enjoyed its quiet, as also the rural beauty of the village and the gentle society of the people. There were long winter evenings to be passed in hospitable homes; evenings marked by discussions of slavery or by stories of perils and escapes on the border. Then, in turn, there was the pleasure—not unmixed with a certain wonder and awe—

which was afforded to the villagers by the
presence among them of men of such strik·
ing parts and individuality as were these
followers of John Brown.   It was not every
village that was favored with the society of
a John Henrie Kagi, for instance, a man of
thought and of varied accomplishments—a
stenographer, among other things, and, at
one time, correspondent in Kansas for the
New York Post; or of an Aaron D. Stephens,[1]
a man who had served in the United States
Army, been sentenced by a court-martial to
be shot for assaulting an officer who it was
said was brutally chastising one of the men,
but had escaped and was now enlisted with
Brown under the name of C. Whipple ; or of
a Richard Realf,[2] eloquent, poetic, impetuous;

[1] Aaron D. Stephens was a member of Company F.,
First Dragoons, U. S. Army.   On May 25th, 1855, he, together with three comrades, was sentenced to death for par-
ticipation in what is called in his sentence " a drunken riot
and mutiny against a major of the regiment."   The Court
Martial which passed the sentence convened at Don Fer-
nandez de Taos, New Mexico, where the regiment was
when the mutiny occurred.   Afterwards, on August 9th,
1855, the sentence of death was commuted by President
Pierce to three years at hard labor, under guard, and without pay; but ere this, Stephens had made his escape.

[2] " I am a native of England.   I was born in the year
1834.   I will therefore be twenty-six next June.   I first came
to this country in 1854.   My parents are living now in England.   At the time I left England my father was filling the

claiming to have been the especial protégé of Lady Noel Byron, and suspected of having been mixed up in foreign political troubles ; or of a John Edwin Cook, also poetic, handsome in flowing hair, a masterly penman, lily fingered perhaps, but none the less of great courage and the crack shot of the company.

It was not all play for Brown's men while in Springdale. Brown himself never for a moment lost sight of the great end which he had in view. Aaron D. Stephens was appointed drill master, and a regular daily routine of military study and drill insisted upon. Five o clock was the rising hour ; immediately after breakfast study was begun and continued until nine or ten o'clock ; books were then laid aside and the men drilled in the school of the soldier on the broad sward to the east of the Maxon house. In the afternoon a sort of combined gymnastics and

position which he now fills, namely, an officer of the English rural police. My father was a blacksmith at one time. That trade he learned himself. He was a peasant, which means an agricultural laborer. I had been a protégé of Lady Noel Byron. I had disagreed with Lady Byron on account of some private matters, which it is not necessary to explain here, but which rendered me desirous of finding some other place in which to dwell. Moreover my instincts were democratic and republican or at least anti-monarchical. Therefore I came to America."—*Richard Realf in his testimony before Senator Mason's Committee on the John Brown affair.*

company manœuvers were practiced, the object
of which apparently was to inure the men to
the strain of running, jumping, vaulting,
and firing in different and difficult atti-
tudes.[1]   Among other exercises was a sword
drill which was performed with long wooden
sabres, one of which—the one used by Owen
Brown—is still preserved in the Maxon
family.   Tuesday and Friday evenings were
set apart for the proceedings of a mock legislature which had been organized.   One of
the sons of Mr. William Maxon remembers
that he served in this honorable body in the
capacity of the member from Cedar county.
The sessions were held either in the large sit-
ting-room of the Maxons, or in the larger
room of the district school building, a mile
and a half away.   There were a speaker, a
clerk of the House, and regular standing
committees.   Bills were introduced, referred,
reported back, debated with intense earnest-
ness and no little ability, and finally brought

[1] Forbes' Manual was used in these drills—especially
that part of it devoted to guerrilla warfare.   Paragraph 57
of the Manual reads as follows: "The irregular troops
cannot be expected to attain a high degree of military instruction; nevertheless the foot guerrilla should with haste,
and even hurry, be practiced in forming single and double
files . . . in the use of the knife, of fire-arms; also to
creep along the ground, to climb and to hide and to form
the chain of skirmishers."

to vote.   Kagi was the keenest debater, and
Realf and Cook orators of very considerable
powers.   The other evenings of the week
were passed by each one according to his
fancy.   There were the good substantial home-
steads of the Painters, the Lewises, the Var-
neys, the Gills, that could be visited ; or
Richard Realf had consented to address the
Lyceum at Pedee, and all Springdale was
going to hear him ; this in part for the pleasure there was in listening to so good a
speaker, but more perhaps because of the
anti-slavery views to which in all probability
he would give utterance, to the amazement
and scandal of the Pedeeites who were strong
Democrats.

It is perhaps not surprising that, under
conditions such as these, some of the hardy
fellows of Brown's command should have
been visited by thoughts of love. All were bach-
elors, and, moreover, all were young: Kagi,
twenty-three ;   Cook, twenty-three or four ;
Realf, twenty-three ; Stephens, twenty-seven ;
Parsons, twenty-two ; Leeman, eighteen ;
Tidd, twenty-five or six ; Moffat, thirty ;
Owen Brown twenty-nine or thirty. Stephens
and Cook and Parsons gave unmistakable
proofs of the birth of the tender passion
within them.   And even Owen Brown, who

seems to have been a bachelor by determination and from principle and who never married, went so far as to divulge the fact that there was one maiden near Springdale whom he would marry, if he ever married at all, but to whom, out of abundant caution, he had resolved, never even to speak.

Brown himself did not remain at Springdale throughout the winter, but soon pushed on East to find and send back Forbes, to raise money, and to confer with Gerritt Smith, Sanborn, Parker and others. But before going he took time earnestly to consult with his friends, Gill, Maxon and Painter. What he disclosed to them of his plans and purposes is substantially what he afterwards (on February 22d, 1858,) disclosed to Gerritt Smith and F. B. Sanborn at Peterboro, New York, namely, a scheme of invasion of Virginia. He also, it seems, intimated (at least to Gill) that the point of invasion would be Harper's Ferry.[1] Gill, Maxon, and Painter,

[1] "Some time toward Spring. John Brown came to my house one Sunday afternoon. He informed me that he wished to have some private talk with me; we went into the parlor. He then told me his plans for the future. He had not then decided to attack the Armory at Harper's Ferry, but intended to take some fifty to one hundred men into the hills near the Ferry and remain there until he could get together quite a number of slaves, and then take what conveyances were needed to transport the negroes and their

as afterwards Smith and Sanborn, tried to dissuade him from attempting this hardy enterprise. Mr. Maxon's sons say that, on more than one occasion, their father sat up late into the night with Brown contending with him on the practicability and utility of his scheme. But he was inflexible. He not only had all faith in his little band, pronouncing every one of them a brave man, but believed himself to be the especial instrument of God for the destruction of slavery.

There were other incidents of John Brown's brief stay in Springdale. The following is one of them. One day he was sitting in the house of Mr. Griffith Lewis. Mrs. Lewis sat near by. Her youngest daughter—a school-girl—took a pair of scissors, and, standing behind

families to Canada. And in a short time after the excitement had abated, to make a strike in some other Southern State; and to continue on making raids, as opportunity offered, until slavery ceased to exist. I did my best to convince him that the probabilities were that all would be killed. He said that, as for himself, he was willing to give his life for the slaves. He told me repeatedly, while talking, that he believed he was an instrument in the hands of God through which slavery would be abolished. I said to him: 'You and your handful of men cannot cope with the whole South.' His reply was: 'I tell you, Doctor, it will be the beginning of the end of slavery.' He also told me that but two of his men, Kagi and Stephens, knew what his intentions were."—*From Letter of Dr. H. C. Gill, dated June 1st, 1892.*

Brown's chair, lifted them as if to cut a lock from his hair, at the same time casting an enquiring glance at her mother. " John Brown," said Mrs. Lewis, "my daughter wishes a lock of thy hair." " Well, she can have it," said Brown, " but I would advise her to burn it." It was not burned, and is still in the possession of the daughter—a valued keepsake.

At the time John Brown's men were staying at Springdale, there were living with their mother in the village, in a quaint frame house yet standing, two young men of strong character, Edwin and Barclay Coppoc. Edwin was twenty-four years old and Barclay twenty. Barclay, being in danger from consumption, had found it necessary to travel, and for a time had served with a Company of liberators in Kansas. They both took much interest in Brown, his men and his cause, and at length enlisted under his leadership.

On April 27th, Brown returned from the East with some funds in hand and more promised, and gave orders for the expedition to move. He wrote to his wife : " We start from here to-day, and shall write you again when we stop, which will be in two or three days." The immediate destination of the band proved to be Chatham, Canada West. The leave-taking between them and the people of Springdale was one of tears. Ties which had been knitting through many weeks were sundered, and not only so, but the natural sorrow at parting was intensified by the consciousness of all that the future was full of hazard for Brown and his followers. Before quitting the house and home of Mr. Maxon where they had spent so long a time, each of Brown's band wrote his name in pencil on the wall of the parlor, where the writing still can be seen by the interested traveler. The part of the wall where the names are written is protected by a door opening against it, and to this cause, doubtless, is chiefly due the preservation of the writing for more than thirty years. The old house itself, which was built of cement and gravel in 1839, is still standing, but for a good while has been unoccupied. It is falling into decay, yet is full of interest. I went to see it not many weeks ago accompanied by a son of Mr. William Maxon. The boundaries of the old drill ground near by still can be made out. The old evergreen trees still shade the structure on all sides. The path that formerly led to the front door is grass-grown and obscured, but still can be traced between the two large lilac bushes that to-day stand on either side of it, as they did when Brown's band first approached the house.

The large west front room in which the mock legislature, as well as informal talks of the band, were held, is well preserved; also the commodious kitchen where the meals were served by Mrs. Maxon,—a woman as resolute and uncompromising in her abolitionism as was her husband in his, and who still lives at an advanced age,—and the small attic bedroom in which Owen Brown used to practice short-hand which he was learning from Kagi, and where all the band slept. The cellar of this old house is hardly less interesting than the house itself; for in it, in the days of slavery, Mr. Maxon constantly was keeping hid small parties of fugitive negroes from Missouri. The fire-place by which it was made comfortable in winter, may still be seen.

The men who left Springdale with Brown, besides those who originally had come there with him, were George B. Gill and Steward Taylor—the latter a young Canadian. The Coppocs did not go with him, but were intending to join him soon. On reaching Chatham, Canada West, arrangements were made for holding a Constitutional Convention. Richard Realf wrote to Dr. Gill on April 30th: "Here, [at Chatham] we intend to remain till we have perfected our plans, which will be in about ten days or two weeks, after which

we start for *China*. Yesterday and this morning we have been very busy in writing to Gerritt
Smith, and Wendell Phillips and others of like
kin to meet us in this place on Saturday, the
8th of May, to adopt our Constitution, decide
a few matters, and bid us good-bye. Then
we start. . . . . . The signals and mode of
writing are (the old man [John Brown] in-
forms me) all arranged. . . . . . Remember
me to all who know our business, but to all
others be dumb as death." The Convention
assembled on the 8th of May, adopted the Constitution which has been so much wondered
at and derided, and two days later proceeded
to name officers for the government which had
been established. John Brown was named
as Commander in Chief, Kagi, as Secretary of
War, Richard Realf, as Secretary of State,
and George B. Gill, as Secretary of the Treas-
ury. But meantime Hugh Forbes had been
busy writing letters to Sanborn, Dr. Howe
and Theodore Parker in which he threatened
to tell all that he knew of Brown's plans. He
even wrote to Senators Sumner and Wilson,
and managed to get an interview with Senator
Seward at Washington. In view of these facts,
it was decided by Gerritt Smith and Brown's
friends in Massachusetts (with the exception
of Mr. T. W. Higginson who protested against

the decision) that the scheme must for the
present be abandoned. Brown, therefore, was
hastily summoned to meet George L. Stearns,
and others of his friends in New York, in
which city he arrived about May 22d. On
May 24th, a consultation was held in Boston
between Smith, Parker, Howe, Stearns, and
Sanborn, and the conclusion reached that
Brown must immediately go to Kansas and
should be provided with money to that end,
and, for the present to, no other. On May
31st, Brown called on Higginson, expressed
his disappointment at the action taken by
Smith, Parker and the others, and plainly
intimated that, were it not for his dependence
upon these gentlemen for money, he would
proceed to the consummation of his Virginia
undertaking, Forbes or no Forbes.

Brown's men were compelled to separate
by this new turn in affairs and to find, as best
they could, a temporary means of livelihood.
Brown himself, his indomitable second in
command, Kagi, and Charles P. Tidd went to
Kansas, where they were soon joined by
Stephens. Realf was sent to New York to
stop the mouth of Forbes ; Gill came back to
Iowa ; Owen Brown, Parsons, and Moffat
went to Ohio ; Cook, after some little time
spent in Ohio, went forward to Harper's

Ferry, Virginia, where he carefully took note of everything ; studied the formation of the country and ascertained the whereabouts of the dwellings of prominent persons.   It thus becomes apparent that, at least by this time, Harper's Ferry had been definitely selected by Brown as the point of invasion, and that Cook had been so apprised

The homesickness which beset the hearts of the little company, after their separation from Springdale friends and scenes, is made plain by the following letter from John E. Cook, which has not before been in print.

CHATHAM, CANADA WEST, May 6th, 1858.
MY DEAR SISTERS :[1]

I feel lonely here, and having at present nothing to do, I have concluded to let my pen follow my thoughts, and so I am writing to you.   I am here, but my mind and heart are with you in your happy home. . . . . . I wish to write to my parents, sisters and brother, but dare not at present on account of future plans.   For, should they know that I am stopping here, it would awaken suspicion as to the cause of it.   And then, besides, Mr. B. [John Brown] says he had rather we would not write until we leave here ; for which request he has good reasons. . . . . . Time hangs heavily on my hands while waiting here ; and there is but

[1] The young women of one of the Springdale families in which Cook had become intimate.

one thing that keeps me from being absolutely unhappy, and that is the consciousness that I am in the path of duty. I long for the 10th of May [the day fixed upon for the final proceedings at Chatham] to come. I am anxious to leave this place ; to have my mind occupied with the great work of our mission. [The Virginia enterprise was frequently referred to by Brown's men as a mission.] For, amid the bustling, busy scenes of the camp, I should be less lonely and therefore more happy than at present. I did not know till I left you that there was so much of selfishness in my nature; that there would be so great a struggle between the desires of a selfish heart and my manifest duty. But so it is. We do not know ourselves till we are tried in the great crucible of time and circumstances. . . . . .

The prospects of our cause are growing brighter and brighter. Through the dark gloom of the future I fancy I can almost see the dawning light of Freedom ; . . . . . that I can almost hear the swelling anthem of Liberty rising from the millions who have but just cast aside the fetters and the shackles that bound them. But ere that day arrives, I fear that we shall hear the crash of the battle shock and see the red gleaming of the cannon's lightning.

By the way, the Lecompton Bill has passed both Houses, and poor Kansas is admitted into the Union as a slave State. You see, therefore, that my prophecy in regard to that matter is fulfilled.

Well, taking all things into consideration, I am not sorry that it has passed, for it will help us in our work. I shall expect to hear of some hard battles in Kansas.

Enclosed you will find a few flowers that I gathered in my rambles about town. They are the earliest flowers that bloom in this region. Accept them with my best wishes. . . . . . Realf asks to be remembered and sends his best wishes for your welfare. We are all well save hard colds. . . . . .

I remain, as ever, your affectionate brother,

J. E. COOK.

P. S. Please direct to me in care of E. A. Fobes, Lindenville, Ashtabula County, Ohio.

Write immediately,

J. E. COOK.

As soon as Brown began to get distinct intimations from his friends in the east that funds would not be forthcoming for the immediate prosecution of his Virginia scheme, he made known the fact to his band, and to some of them, who had gone to Ohio to find work, wrote the two letters printed below. These letters are not to be found in any life of Brown, nor, I think, in any of the magazine articles about him which have appeared.

CHATHAM, CANADA WEST, 18th of May, 1858.
Dear Friends, All :—

The letter of George [B. Gill], of the 13th inst., is received, by which we learn of your safe arrival; also that you do not find the best encouragement about business.   I will only inquire if you, any of you, think the difficulties you have experienced so far, are sufficient to discourage a man ?   I should not hesitate for one moment to inquire out some good farmer's family in the country and say to them [that] I was travelling to Pennsylvania, or some other part East ; that I had got out of money, and wanted work for a while ; that I did not wish to engage for a long time until I could see whether I could give satisfaction or not, and whether I should like to stay or not. I would offer to work a few days for my board, and just what more a respectable man would be willing to give me, on trial. In that way I would save my board bill, at any rate, and be making acquaintances and be finding out about chances and wages.   I would not be afraid of spoiling myself by working hard on such conditions for a few days.   I and three others were in exactly such a fix in the spring of 1817, between the seaside and Ohio, in a time not only of extreme scarcity of money, but of the greatest distress for want of provisions known during the nineteenth century.   It was the next year after the "cold summer," as it has ever since been called ; and, would you believe it? some of that company are on their legs yet.   I would say I was going to Pittsburgh, Pa., or to Bedford, or to Chambers-

burg, or to some other large town in that direction.
We shall all be obliged to hold on somewhere
until we can get more funds, and until we can
know better how to act. We here are busy getting
information and making other preparations. I
believe no time has yet been lost. Owing to the
panic on the part of some of our Eastern friends,
we may be compelled to hold on for months yet.
But what of that? What I am most afraid of is
that some of you will be in great distress to show
your arms, or to show yourselves to be something
uncommon, or something to gain notice, or to get
some help to keep the knowledge you have of
your own business. I am sure that "where there
is a will there is a way." I am negotiating about
that way, as fast as possible. I would like to have
you keep track of each other, so that all can col-
lect when best, and do not spoil any work by
impatience. You shall be posted up, as soon as
anything comes to post up with. It is all well
that you are not here; this is no place for you.
You may see some or all of us soon ; or you may
not for some days. I want all to see this who can.
You will get something more soon.

Your Friend.

I wrote as above because of the vein of blue
your letter seems to contain."

To this letter the following postscript was
appended by Richard Realf :

P. S. Dear George, and dear friends, all:

Last night I received the letter alluded to in

"Uncle's" together with the postage stamps, for which I thank Owen. I do not wonder at your impatience; it is natural that men who have cut themselves loose from all other associations, purposely to devote themselves to a great and worthy end, should be chafed by difficulties and delays. Yet in the exact proportion of our true devotion to this cause, will be the true adherence unto it, though months and years may intervene before we can make our hope a reality. Having devoted our lives to this matter, our lives necessarily belong to it—no moment of time is ours—it is all its : a little earlier or later does not matter; for remember that "they also serve who only stand and wait." "Instant in season and out of season," is the mark of true manhood; perhaps this delay was meant to test us—to try, not our intensity of feeling, but our calmness of endurance. "He who endureth unto the end," you know; and the end of this cloud will come; perhaps it is very nigh unto us. Let us believe in God. I know he will not let his work go unfinished. Much love from all to all. No letters from our friends in Iowa. Look up! the darkest hour is just before the dawn. I will write you again at more length soon. Truly, R. R."

CHATHAM, CANADA WEST, May 21st, 1858.
Dear Son [Owen Brown] and other friends, all :

The letters of three of your number are received, dated on the 16th. by which we learn the difficulties you find in getting employment. It appears that all but three have managed to stop their board bills ; and I do hope that the balance will follow the man-like and noble example of patience and perseverance set them by the others, instead of being either discouraged or out of humor. The weather is so wet here that no work can be obtained. I have only received $15 as yet from the East; and such has been the effect of the course taken by F. [Forbes] on our eastern friends that I have some fears that we shall be compelled to delay further action for the present. They urge us to do so ; promising liberal assistance after a while. I am in hourly expectation of help sufficient to pay off our bills here and to take us on to Cleveland to see and advise with you, which we shall do at once when we get the means. Suppose we do have to defer our direct efforts ; shall great and noble minds either indulge in useless complaints, or fold their arms in discouragement, or sit in idleness when at least we may avoid losing much gained? It is in times of difficulty that men show what they are. It is in such times that men mark themselves. "He that endureth unto the end," the same shall get his reward. Are our difficulties sufficient to make us give up one of the noblest enterprises in which men were ever engaged? Write James M. Bell,

Your Sincere Friend.

Cook's efforts to find work, in accordance with Brown's advice as given above, are told by him in the following letter to his Iowa correspondents. The penmanship of this letter is not a little remarkable, being not only perfect throughout, but in part executed with such minuteness as hardly to be legible except by means of a lens.

LAWRENCE, KANSAS, June 6th, 1858.

My Dear Sisters :

I am, as you see by the date of this, still in Ohio.[1] How long I shall remain here is uncertain. But I hope not long, for I am tired of this delay. There are two causes which keep us here. The first and most important one is the want of funds to take us to our destination. Those who promised to raise the money at the shortest notice have failed to do so. So we are detained. And, in order that the Old Gentleman [John Brown] may save the little he has got, we have separated, and are most of us working for our board. Times are so hard here that we can get no chance to work for wages, and so we have concluded to do the next best thing we can do—get our living by our labor. This, for me, is something new, and it goes rather hard ; but we feel that it is in a good cause and so we take it patiently. It is the best test that could be made of our fidelity to the cause in which we have engaged. Of course we all regret our delay, and the alternative it involves, yet no one has shrunk from accepting it, viz : Hard labor

[1] Above the words, " Lawrence, Kansas," in the original letter, is written in lead pencil, " Orange Centre, Ohio," at which place Cook in fact was.

for the mere pittance of our food[1] till such time as we can raise funds enough to take us onward to the chosen field of our labor.

I am with a farmer by the name of Hayward, in this place. I wrote on to Kansas two days ago, to

[1] As revealing still more clearly the straitened circumstances of Brown's band after the separation at Chatham, Canada West, the following letter from Luke F. Parsons to George B. Gill is here printed for the first time:

CLEVELAND [OHIO], May 26th, 1858.
Dear Friend George:

I have just received your letter for, or directed to, A. Stephens. Why did you not direct to me? I came very near not opening it. . . . . . I will immediately write to Cook, who is at Orange, and not doing anything as yet. He intends to get up a writing school, but it is not at all likely that he can do so these hard times. Tidd, Whipple and Taylor are working among the Shakers for fifty cents a day. . . . . . Taylor told a hard story of suffering, privations and fatigue. He laid out one night with another poor devil like himself. While I write Owen [Brown] comes in. He is going to leave the place where he is, for the old man [his employer] is so cross that they cannot agree. He will take "French leave." He thinks of going to his brother's in Akron. Have not heard one word from anyone but Moffat. He is at home and is going to Lindenville to-day. He talks rather blue. I am afraid that we have lost him. . . . . . I don't get a d——d thing to do yet. To-day I went to the City prison, but I don't think I should like to board there. It is very necessary that some one stay here to attend to the P. O. and to watch for some of the rest. But to-morrow my board for one week will be due, and after paying that I shall only have money enough to pay one week more. Write soon again; tell me all the particulars. . . . . . Keep a stiff upper lip. Set your face Zionward. Be sure and write immediately. From your Brother,

L. F. PARSONS.

see what chance there would be for the sale of some of my property there. [Cook, before joining Brown, had been engaged in the real estate business at Lawrence, Kansas, with a man by the name of Bacon: the firm name was Cook & Bacon.]

If I can effect a sale we will leave here immediately. But I do not wish to give it away or to dispose of it for one fourth its value. You can see from this that our way, even thus early, is not all sunshine. Then there is another cause of delay. One of those entrusted with our secret [Forbes] has behaved rather treacherously. But to what extent his treachery goes, I do not as yet know. However, that would not keep us back, even for a moment, if we had the means to carry us on to the place of our destination. But we live in hopes, and are looking for the dawn of a brighter morrow. God grant that our waiting may not be long!

I am lonely here. . . . . . My thoughts are ever going back to the happy hours I have spent with my friends in Springdale. . . . . . I came as a stranger; I was treated as a friend and brother; and in turn you have my undying gratitude and affection. The parting hour came; higher, holier duties called me, and I left you — probably forever. . . . . .

But I must close these hasty and imperfect lines. Please give my love to sisters Phebe, Sarah and Agnes. I should have given them a share in this letter, only as they do [not] know our destination, I did not know as it would be best to inform them yet. You can, however, read this page to them, if you like, as the sentiments it contains are theirs as well as yours. The rest of it I shall expect will be kept a secret from all, save those who know our secret. Please write me a long letter on receipt of this. I shall expect either a long letter from you collectively, or else a good one from each one of you. As I do not know how long I shall remain here, please direct to me in care of E. A. Fobes, Lindenville, Ashtabula County, Ohio. Give my kind regards to Fanny Jones, and also to all inquiring friends in Springdale. I am stopping at Orange Centre, a place about fourteen miles from Cleveland. I shall, however, date this, Lawrence, Kansas, for reasons which you will readily guess and appreciate. Esther and Elvira will please read this, and then send it as soon as possible to Laura, who in turn will send it to Eliza. Accept with these lines my best wishes and most fervent prayers for your present and eternal welfare, and may God speed you in joy upon your way. From him who here subscribes himself your brother in affection,

JOHN EDWIN COOK.

Cook's next letter to his Springdale correspondents, and the last that I have been able to find written before the Harper's Ferry affair, bears date, Harper's Ferry, Va., July 3d, 1858. It is in a rhapsodical strain, to which Cook was a good deal inclined, and contains nothing of interest.

The story of Brown's raid into Missouri,
after his return to Kansas, in 1858, is well
known.   Suffice it to say, that on this raid he
took from their owners a dozen slaves with
whom, aided by Kagi and Stephens, amid
great perils he made good his escape into
Nebraska, and thence to Tabor in Iowa.
Here, contrary to his expectation and contrary to the whole former attitude of the
people, he was not welcomed, but, at a public
meeting called for the purpose, severely rep-
rimanded as a disturber of the peace and
safety of the village.   Effecting a hasty departure from Tabor, and taking advantage of
the protection offered by a few friendly families on the way, he and his party of fugitives
came, on February 20th, 1859, to Grinnell,
Iowa, where they were cordially received by
the Hon. J. B. Grinnell who entertained
them in his house.   Brown's next stop was
made at Springdale, which place he reached
on February 25th.   Here the fugitives were dis-
tributed among the Quaker families for
safety and rest before continuing their journey to Canada.   But soon rumors were afloat
of the coming of the United States Marshal,
and it became necessary to secure for the
negroes railroad transportation to Chicago.
Kagi and Stephens, disguised as sportsmen,

walked to Iowa City, enlisted the services of Mr. William Penn Clark, an influential anti-slavery citizen of that place, and by his efforts, supplemented by those of Hon. J. B. Grinnell, a freight car was got and held in readiness at West Liberty.

The negroes were then brought down from Springdale (distant but six miles) and, after spending a night in a grist mill near the rail-way station, were ready to embark. It is an interesting scene that was beheld by the people of West Liberty this March day of 1859 on which John Brown was loading his car with dusky passengers for Canada and Freedom. Huddled together in a little group near the track, stand the negroes, patient, wondering. Near them, leaning on their Sharp's rifles, heavy revolvers in their belts, on the alert, stand Kagi and Stephens. In a few minutes the freight car which has been got with so much trouble, and by not a little prevarication as to the use to which it is to be put, is pushed by a crowd of men down the side-track to a point convenient for the load-ing. Brown mounts into it and shakes the door and lays hold of the sides that he may judge of its capacity for resistance in case of attack. Clean straw is then brought to him which he spreads over the floor. After this,

the negro babes and small children, of whom
there are several, are handed up to him and
he tenderly deposits them among the straw.
The older negroes are next helped in, and all
is ready. The passenger train on the Chicago
and Rock Island Road rolls in from the West.
For a moment there is suspense. Is the
United States Marshal on board ? No ! The
train draws out from the station, stops, backs
down on the side-track and is coupled to the
freight car. Kagi and Stephens get into one
of the passenger coaches, and John Brown is
leaving Iowa for the last time.

Events rapidly transpired. On reaching
Chicago, Brown and his party were taken in
friendly charge by Allan Pinkerton, the
famous detective, and started for Detroit.
On March 10th, they were in Detroit and
practically at their journey's end. From
there Brown went to Peterboro, New York ;
then to Concord, Massachusetts, where he
again spoke in the town hall, making a deep
impression on Henry D. Thoreau ; then to
Boston, where he arrived on May 9th. He
left Boston, on June 3d, for Ohio, and, on
June 30th, was at Chambersburg, Pennsylvania.
On July 3d, he and his two sons, Owen and
Oliver, were at Harper's Ferry where they
met Cook. On July 15th, Brown wrote to

Edwin and Barclay Coppoc at Springdale, requesting that they join him at Chambersburg, Pennsylvania. They required no second summons. On July 25th, Barclay said to his mother: "We are going to start for Ohio to-day." "Ohio!" said the mother, "I believe you are going with old Brown. When you get the halters round your necks will you think of me?"

After the departure of Edwin and Barclay Coppoc, almost nothing concerning the movements of John Brown came to the ears of anybody in Springdale till October 17th or 18th. Then a thrill of terror shot through the community. A telegraphic despatch in some newspaper stated that a crazy old man and some twenty followers had seized the United States Arsenal at Harper's Ferry, Virginia, and were holding their assailants, Virginia chivalry and United States Marines, at bay. On October 20th, C. W. Moffat, who by this time had returned to Springdale and was there making ready to join Brown, received the following letter from Kagi, written the night before the foray:

We hear that a warrant has been issued to search our house here [the house on the Kennedy farm]; so we have got to make the strike eight days sooner than the date fixed in our previous notice to you. Start at once. Study map.[1] We will try to hold out till you reach us.

JOHN H. KAGI.
Secretary of the Constitutional Convention.

Little by little the details of the affair came to light. It was learned that Kagi, Leeman, and Taylor had been shot and killed; that John Brown, Edwin Coppoc, and Stephens had been captured; that Owen Brown, Barclay Coppoc, Cook, and Tidd had escaped; and that Richard Realf had not been of the party making the foray, having gone to England in the summer of 1858,[2] then to France, and was now somewhere in the southern States. After a fortnight further news came: John E. Cook had been captured. Owen Brown, Barclay Coppoc, and Tidd were still at liberty. On November 8th or 10th, Mrs.

[1] The map referred to was of the public road leading from Harper's Ferry to the Kennedy farm. It was furnished so that Moffat would not have to enquire his way to the rendezvous.

[2] On July 28, 1858, Richard Realf had written to George B. Gill as follows:

Room 10, 16 Wall Street, New York City.
DEAR BRO. GEORGE: I have received news from England. My mother is very sick. If I can arrange matters, I shall run across to see her. If I go, I shall be back in *time*. Indeed I am somewhat fearful that we shall not commence before next spring. Truly Your Bro.,
RICHARD.

Ann Coppoc received a letter from her son, Edwin. It was dated Charlestown, Va., November 5, 1859, and told briefly the fact of his capture. It ended with these words: "Give my love to Briggs' and Maxons' folks and to all other inquiring friends, for [of] such I feel that I have a large circle; and I trust that what I have done will not make them enemies. My love to all the family. No more. Edwin Coppoc." About the same time, Dr. H. C. Gill received from Coppoc a letter, in which he said: "Whatever may be our fate, rest assured that we will not shame our dead companions by a shrinking fear." After his trial, on December 10th, Coppoc wrote to Mr. John H. Painter: "To-day we have received a box of knick-knacks from Philadelphia, and some of the citizens here send us in a pie now and then; so you may know that we live fat, but it is only fattening us up for the gallows—rather poor consolation." Finally, on December 13th, he sent these lines to his uncle in Ohio: "I have heard my sentence passed; my doom is sealed. But two brief days between me and eternity. At the end of these two days I shall stand upon the scaffold to take my last look at earthly scenes. But that scaffold has but little dread for me, for I honestly believe that I am innocent of any crime justifying such punishment."

One farewell message penned by Edwin Coppoc is of extraordinary interest. It is in these few, yet sufficient, words: "Dear Elza, Farewell. Edwin Coppoc." The person to whom the message is addressed is one of the sons of Mr. William Maxon, but he did not know of the message or receive it until Edwin Coppoc had been in his grave for more than twenty-six years. The facts are these: When Coppoc left Springdale to join Brown at Harper's Ferry, he took with him an ambrotype picture of his friend, Elza Maxon. The picture was contained in a small covered case from which it could easily be removed. Just before his execution, Coppoc took out the picture and wrote on the surface of that part of the case against which the back of the picture rested the words above quoted; thinking naturally enough that, when his personal effects were sent home, the picture would be returned to Maxon, and sooner or later the message be found. But, as it chanced, Mrs. Coppoc never returned the picture and it remained in her hands until she died. It was then, with some other things deemed rubbish, thrown into a corner of the old Coppoc house and forgotten. One day when idly looking through the house, Maxon came upon the case, opened it, found the picture, and, impelled by some strange curiosity, removed it. The message had come at last.

But meantime, what of Barclay Coppoc? He got to Springdale on December 17th, after a journey of a month through the mountains of Maryland and Pennsylvania, the exciting particulars of which have been narrated by Owen Brown[1] in a paper printed in the *Atlantic Monthly* for March, 1877. He was thin and haggard and nearly exhausted. The welcome that met him was warm ; it was tearful as well. On the day before that on which he came, his brother, Edwin, and John E. Cook had died upon the scaffold. Nor was he safe from pursuit. So spent were his powers, however, that his friends at Springdale resolved to protect him at any cost, and banded themselves together in a military organization to that end. Nightly guard was kept around the Coppoc house, and at a preconcerted signal all were to assemble. Among

[1] The death of Owen Brown occurred in 1888, near Pasadena, California, where he was living with his brother, Jason, and his sister, Ruth. The funeral services were conducted by the Quaker preacher of the locality and were attended by a great throng. Among the pall-bearers were the two staunch friends of John Brown at Springdale, John H. Painter and James Townsend, both of whom had removed to California.

those thus enlisted were some who, as on a
certain famous occasion in Pennsylvania,
afforded the unusual spectacle of the close
juxtaposition of a musket and a broad-
brimmed hat.

On the 23d of January, 1860, one C. Camp,
as agent of the State of Virginia, appeared in
Des Moines, Iowa, and served upon Governor
Samuel J. Kirkwood a requisition for Barclay
Coppoc.   For some reason Camp let his
errand become generally known, and immediately steps were taken by the sympathisers
with Coppoc at Des Moines to advise him of
his peril.   The legislature was in session and
a sum of money was hastily raised among the
members.   With it a horseman was hired to
carry to Springdale this message : "Des
Moines, January 24, 1860. Mr. J. H. Painter :
There is an application for young Coppoc
from the Governor of Virginia, and the Governor here will be compelled to surrender
him. If he is in your neighborhood, tell him
to make his escape from the United States.
Your Friend." But Coppoc would not go.
It did not in this instance prove to be necessary that he should, for the requisition was
defective in form, and compliance with it was
refused by Governor Kirkwood on that account.   Later, on February 4th, a second

requisition for Barclay Coppoc was made upon Governor Kirkwood, and being in due form and accompanied by copies of two indictments found against Coppoc by the grand jury of Jefferson County, Virginia, was granted. The necessary papers were put into the hands of the sheriff of Cedar County to be served ; but that functionary skillfully evaded a most ungrateful and dangerous task by going to Springdale and loudly enquiring of everybody whom he met for Barclay Coppoc. He did not find him and made official return that he was not to be found within the limits of Cedar County.

It was now thought best for Coppoc to go to Canada and remain there until the public mind should quiet down. To do this he reluctantly consented, and in disguise and accompanied by a son of Mr. Maxon, he went to Detroit, and from there into Canada. But hearing that Owen Brown, John Brown, Jr., F. J. Merriam, of Massachusetts, and James Redpath were in Ashtabula county, Ohio, he went thither, still accompanied by Maxon, and there, at the little town of Dorset, the six men stayed for three weeks, always heavily armed and never separated. They were at this place on March 16, 1860, the day on which Aaron D. Stephens was hanged. In 1861

Barclay Coppoc enlisted in the Union army and was killed in a railroad wreck at a crossing of the Platte river ; the wreck was caused by the Confederates having partially sawed in two the supports to the bridge.

None of John Brown's band, even in the hour of his extremity, forgot Springdale or the friends there made. John E. Cook wrote to Mr. and Mrs. James Townsend on December 15, 1859: "We struck a blow for the freedom of the slave. We failed, and those who are not already dead must die, and that upon the scaffold. Accept my love, my God-speed, and my last farewell." A fortnight earlier Aaron D. Stephens had written as follows to Mrs. Varney: "I feel perfectly guiltless of the charges brought against me. I have done nothing but what I think is right and just." As for Brown himself, he told Stephens to say for him that he wished to be remembered by all the kind friends at Springdale. "And," adds Stephens, "although his end is drawing nigh, he is as cheerful as if he were in your midst."

NOTE.

Among the answers made by Richard Realf in his examination before Senator Mason's committee are the following: "I formed the acquaintance of John Brown the last of November or the first of December [1857]. I was residing in the city of Lawrence, Kansas, as correspondent of the

Illinois State Journal, edited by Messrs. Bailhache & Baker. I had been and was a radical abolitionist. In November, 1857, John Edwin Cook, recently executed in Virginia, came to my boarding house in Lawrence, bringing me an invitation from John Brown to visit him at a place called Tabor, in Iowa. There I met John Brown. John Brown made known to me to a certain, but not very definite and detailed, degree his intentions. He stated that he purposed to make an incursion into the Southern States, somewhere in the mountainous region of the Blue Ridge and the Alleghanies. From Tabor, where I myself first met John Brown and the majority of the persons forming the white part of his company in Virginia, we passed across the State of Iowa, until we reached Cedar county in that State. We started in December, 1857. It was about the end of December, 1857, or the beginning of January, 1858, when we reached Cedar county, the journey thus consuming about a month of time. We stopped at a village called Springdale in that county, where, in a settlement principally composed of Quakers, we remained. Myself, Mr. Kagi, Mr. Cook, Mr. Stephens, Mr. Tidd, Mr. Leeman, Mr. Moffat, Mr. Parsons, and Mr. Owen Brown, all these being whites, and Mr. Richard Richardson, a colored man whom I met with Brown at Tabor, composed our company. We remained at Springdale from the month — whether it be, I cannot now remember, the latter part of December, 1857, or the beginning of January, 1858,—but from that time up until about the last week in April — a period of nearly three [four] months. We were being drilled a part of the time and receiving military lessons under Mr. Stephens. A part of the time I was lecturing. Brown provided for the support of the company whilst we were there in this way: upon reaching there he, finding himself unable to dispose of the mules and wagons with which he transported us across the State, and unable to get the price he desired for them, left us there to board, the property named to belong to the man who kept us, a price having been agreed upon between himself and Mr. Brown. We boarded with a Mr. Maxon. During our passage across Iowa Brown's plan in regard to an incursion

into Virginia gradually manifested itself. It was a matter
of discussion between us as to the possibility of effecting a
successful insurrection in the mountains, some arguing that
it was, some that it was not; myself thinking and still thinking that a mountainous country is a very fine country for an
insurrection, in which I am borne out by historic evidence
which it is not necessary to state now. Brown expected to
make his incursion into Virginia in the spring of 1858. We
expected Colonel Forbes to be our military instructor, yet
in consequence of a disagreement between himself and John
Brown, the latter wrote us from the East that Forbes would
not become our military instructor and that we should not
expect him. I am inclined to think that the people [of
Springdale] knew nothing at all of our movements, for the
reason that by some we were suspected to be Mormon missionaries. I believe that John Brown had given a man
named Townsend, I cannot remember his first name, a
member of the Society of Friends, some indirect and indefi-
nite hints of his plan. I also think that from the nature of
a conversation which a Mr. Varney (also residing in the
immediate neighborhood, and being also a Quaker,) had
with myself, someone must have given him some hints in
regard to the same matter; but neither of these people
were evidently, from the tone of their conversation, possessed of any definite information in regard to the matter.
Our military training was conducted principally behind the
house of Mr. Maxon, it being generally understood in the
place where we were boarding, in the vicinity, and round
about that we were thus studying tactics and being thus
drilled in order to return to Kansas, to prosecute our en-
deavors to make Kansas a free State. We had our private
arms. John E. Cook had his own private arms. I had
my pair of Colt's revolvers. Brown did not, to my knowledge, furnish any of his company with arms. I met the
people composing this company at Tabor. All of them had
been engaged in Kansas warfare. Everybody at that period
in Kansas went armed. All of the company whom I have
named as having gone to Springdale accompanied Brown
to Chatham, and two others, a young man named George

B. Gill, who resided at Springdale, who had learned of our plans, from whom I do not know, but I suppose from John Brown, inasmuch as he never manifested any desire to accompany us anywhere until the return of John Brown; and another young man named Stewart [Steward] Taylor, the latter of whom was killed at Harper's Ferry, and the former of whom, so far as I have been able to learn, was not present at the incursion.

MASCOUTIN

MASCOUTIN.

A REMINISCENCE OF THE NATION OF FIRE.

MASCOUTIN (or Muscatine, as the spelling and pronunciation now are,) is the one town of this name in the United States of America. It is situated in the state of Iowa, on the Mississippi river, at the vertex of the great bend into the state which a glance at the map will show that the river makes. High and picturesque bluffs overhang the river, and on these the town of Muscatine is built. Southwest of the town is a low, flat, sandy tract containing nearly forty thousand acres—an island by natural formation, being separated from the Illinois shore on the east by the river, and from the Iowa shore on the west by a narrow, winding slough. The name of this island is also Muscatine ; and it is worthy of remark that it bore this name long before the town of Muscatine was founded, and indeed from a period altogether remote and indeterminate.

The derivation of this name Mascoutin, or Muscatine, has ever been a question of interest for local antiquarians. That it is Indian nobody has doubted ; but with re-

gard to its meaning and with regard to the
tribe or band who first applied it to the island
under consideration, opinions have differed.
In 1852 the editor of one of the daily papers
printed in Muscatine wrote to Antoine le Claire,
at Davenport, Iowa, for a definition of the word
Muscatine.   Le Claire was of French-Indian
extraction, and in pioneer days had been the
official interpreter for the United States government in its dealings with the Indians of
eastern Iowa, chiefly the Sac and Fox tribes ;
he therefore was deemed competent to define
this word.   His reply to the question asked
was that Muscatine " is a sort of combination
of an Indian and French word : mus-quo-ta,
the Indian word, means ' prairie'; the French
added the termination tine to mus-quo-ta,
and the compound word musquo, or musqui-
tine, means ' little prairie.'   The Indian word
menis means ' island,' ashcota means ' fire,'
musquaw means ' red.'   The Indians used to
call the island Mus-quo-ta-menis, which means
' prairie island.'"

Le Claire's definition never has been
entirely satisfactory to Muscatine antiquarians.   They have objected to it on poetic
grounds among others.   For years after, as
doubtless during an untold period before, the
town of Muscatine was founded, (1839)

immense fires would sweep over Muscatine island in the autumn, denuding it of the tall grass—grass as tall as a mounted man—with which its soil was covered. "Now, what more fitting," these antiquarians have contended, "than that the name Muscatine should signify burning or fire island? What more likely, furthermore, than that the Indians, impressed with the magnificent and terrible spectacle of the writhing, sweeping flames, should call the spot, where these flames were as regularly recurrent as the seasons, by some name significant of them? Finally, in addition to all else," say the antiquarians, "Antoine le Claire himself, although defining the word Musquotamenis as prairie island, states the meaning of the Indian word ashcota to be fire, and the meaning of the word musquaw to be 'red.' A philological support is therefore suggested even by Le Claire for the argument we make in favor of the meaning, burning or fire island." One can but be impressed with the force of the reasoning.

But there is a way by which more nearly to reach a solution of this problem of the meaning of the word Mascoutin, or Muscatine ; and not only so, but of the no less difficult problem : What tribe or band of Indians originally gave this name to the island. In the year 1669, Father Claude Allouez, a Jesuit priest, came to Green Bay, in what is now the state of Wisconsin, for the purpose of establishing a mission. While there he ascended the Fox river, passing through the territory occupied by the Sacs and Foxes, and came at length to an Indian town at the west of Lake Winnebago, containing a population of some three thousand souls. This town was Mascoutin (aboriginal Muscatine), or the village of the Mascoutins—a distinct Indian tribe. It was situated, we are told, "on the crown of a hill ; while, all around, the prairie stretched beyond the sight, interspersed with groves and belts of tall forest." Moreover, it was a palisaded town ; that is to say, a town encircled by a row of posts set close together in the ground, against which, on the inner side, heavy sheets of bark had been fastened. As early as 1615 the tribe of the Mascoutins were inhabitants of the country west and southwest of Lake Huron, now southern Michigan, where they had some thirty towns. But from this region they were driven in 1642 or 1643 by the Neutral Nation, so called, their immediate neighbors on the east, and thereafter were to be found in the Fox river region. "Last summer," says the *Relation des Hurons* of 1643, in allusion to the expulsion of the Mascoutins from the Lake Huron country, " two thousand warriors of the Neutral Nation attacked a town of the Nation of Fire, well fortified with a palisade, and defended by nine hundred warriors. They took it after a siege of ten days ; killed many on the spot, and made eight hundred prisoners, men, women, and children. After burning seventy of the best warriors, they put out the eyes of the old men, and cut away their lips, and then left them to drag out a miserable existence." The village of the Mascoutins on Fox river (aboriginal Muscatine) was, it may also be remarked, a point of note and importance. Hither, at one time, came Jean Nicolet, and here he learned from the Mascoutins of the existence of the "great water," the Mississippi. Hither also, in 1659, came the travelers Radisson and Groseilliers ; and concerning the Mascoutins Radisson wrote in his journal: " We made acquaintance with another nation called Escotecke (Mascoutins), wch signified fire, a faire, proper nation ; they weare tall, and big, and very strong. We came there in the spring. When we arrived there were extra-ordinary banquets. There they never had seen men wth beards, because they pull their haires as soone as it comes out ; but much more astonished when they saw our arms, especially our guns, wch they worshipped by blowing smoke of tobacco instead of sacrifice."

Further on, and at a later date, Radisson gives an account of an expedition made by himself and his companion to and down a stream which it seems safe to infer was the Mississippi. His exact words are: "We weare 4 moneths in our voyage wthout doeing anything but goe from river to river. We mett several sorts of people. . . . . By the persuasion of some of them we went into ye great river that divides itself in 2. . . . . It is so called because it has two branches, the one towards the west, the other towards the south, wch we believe runns towards Mexico, by the tokens they gave us." The "branch" spoken of by Radisson as "towards the west" is conjectured by the editor of Radisson's journal, as published in the Wisconsin Historical Collection, to be the upper Iowa river. If so, Radisson and Groseilliers at least journeyed well down towards the site of the present town of Muscatine—and this, moreover, as a direct result of information derived from the Mascoutin Indians.

Now it will be observed—coming to one of the main points of our investigation—that the name Mascoutin, as applied to the Indian tribe of which I have been speaking, is defined by the *Relation des Hurons* of 1643, and by Radisson's journal of 1656 as *fire* nation. To this it may be added that the map of La Salle's colony, finished in 1684 by Jean Baptiste Franquelin, fixes the location of the Mascoutins as on Fox river, and at the same time designates thém as Mascoutins, *Nation du Feu*. But Charlevoix says that the true name of the Mascoutins was Mascoutenec, signifying an open country. He explains the name Mascoutin as a mispronunciation of Mascoutenec by the Pottawattomies, which was taken up and perpetuated by the French. But that there was a word Mascoutin, or something very like it, which, in the Pottawattomie tongue, meant fire, Charlevoix admits.

So here arises again the old dispute. On the one side, contending for the meaning fire nation, we have the early discoverers Radisson, Allouez, Marquette[1] and La Salle, to-

---

[1] *Jes. Rel.* 1670-71. Marquette: "We entered into the river which leads to the Machkoutenech (Mascoutins), called Fire Nation. This is a very beautiful river, without rapids or portages; it flows to the southwest. Along this river are numerous nations: Oumami (Miami), Kikabou (Kickapoo), Machkouteng (Mascoutins), &c. These people are established in a very fine place, where we see beautiful plains, and level country as far as the eye reaches. Their river leads into a great river called Mississippi."

gether with Sagard and Champlain ; while on the other we are confronted by Dablon,[1] Charlevoix, Schoolcraft, and (doubtfully) Parkman.[2] And what, by a sort of amusing perversity, is more perplexing still, the name Mascoutin, as applied to the island in the Mississippi below the present town of Muscatine, is equally pertinent and apropos, be the meaning thereof fire island or prairie island ; for, besides being the flattest and nakedest of prairies, in Indian times this island was wont to be swept yearly by fierce conflagrations.

But what connection is there (coming now to the other leading point of our investigation) between the Mascoutin tribe of Indians on Fox river in what is now the state of Wisconsin, and Mascoutin, or Muscatine, island in the state of Iowa ? How is it even known that Muscatine island originally was Mascoutin island ? Answering the last question

[1] Dablon: "It is beyond this great river that are placed the Illinois, of whom we speak, and from whom are detached those who dwell here with the Fire Nation—Mascoutins. The Fire Nation bears this name erroneously (?) calling themselves Machkoutenech, which signifies ' a land bare of trees' (Muscutah—prairie), such as that which this people inhabit; but because by the change of a few letters (namely scuta, which means fire) from thence it has come that they are called the Fire Nation."

[2] *Wisconsin Historical Collection*, vol. iii. pp. 131–132. Parkman's *Jes. in North America*, p. 436, note.

first, let me quote from the diary of Major
Thomas Forsyth of the United States Army,
kept by him in the year 1819 while on a
voyage up the Mississippi from St. Louis to
the Falls of St. Anthony: "Sunday, June 20th.
Weather still very warm ; had the sail up and
down several times.   Met the Black Thunder
and some followers, all Foxes, going down to
St. Louis in their canoes ; they immediately
returned when they met me.   Encamped a
little above the Iowa river ; eighteen miles
was this day's progress.   Monday, 21st.   We
were off by time this morning ; three Saukies
overtook us on their way from hunting, bound
up to their village on Rocky river ; current
strong to-day, made only twenty-four miles ;
encamped at upper end of Grand Mascoutin."
On the day following he reached Fort Armstrong on Rock Island, having come, he tells
us, "twenty-seven miles from his last stop."
Now the distance from the mouth of the Iowa
river to the head of Muscatine Island is, by
river, at least twenty miles—about what Major
Forsyth guessed to be the distance from his
place of encampment " a little above the Iowa
river" to "the upper end of Grand Mascoutin ";
and the distance from Muscatine Island to
Rock Island is by river twenty-eight miles—
just one mile more than Major Forsyth

guessed it to be. It therefore seems plain that Muscatine Island was known by the name Mascoutin in and before the year 1819.

In answer to the first question—that regarding the connection between the Mascoutin Indians and Mascoutin Island—the following may be said : The Sac and Fox (or more correctly, the Sauk and Musquakie) Indians, as is well known, had inhabited what is now eastern Iowa and western Illinois, near the mouth of Rock river, for seventy or one hundred years before the Black Hawk war of 1831-32. It also is known that early in the eighteenth century the Sac and Fox tribes were denizens of the Fox river region, where were also at that time the Mascoutins. From this region the Sacs and Foxes had migrated to the Rock river region. Is it probable that the Mascoutins, or some of the Mascoutins, migrated with them ? It seem to me that it is. To begin with, the accomplished Indian historian John Gilmary Shea makes the suggestion that the name Musquakie, by which the Fox Indians called themselves, means red land, and may be a corruption of Mash-kooteaki—fire land. If so, Shea thinks that the Foxes comprised the remnant, and bore the name, of the Mascoutins. That the Foxes, or Sacs and Foxes, by the time of their migration to the Rock river region, had absorbed the Mascoutins—not then a numerous people —is, I think, highly probable. That they comprised them—were in fact the remnant of them, seems to me highly improbable. The Foxes were a distinct tribe and had borne the name of Musquakie long prior to their hegira southward. But they readily could have absorbed the Mascoutins : for, first, they were more numerous ; second, they spoke the same tongue[1] ; third, they always had had the Mascoutins for close neighbors and allies[2] ; and fourth, the Mascoutins dropped entirely out of history in the early part of the eighteenth century.[3] Assuming, then, that some of the Mascoutin tribe accompanied the Sacs and Foxes to the mouth of the Rock river, they would have been within twenty-eight miles of the island called Grand Mascoutin in 1819 by Major Forsyth, and today called Muscatine by everybody. That this island, so near

[1] Parkman's *Jes. in North Am.* p. 436, note.

[2] Memoir concerning the peace made by Monsieur de Lignery with the chiefs of the Foxes, etc., June 7, 1726. *Wis. Hist. Col.*, vol. iii. p. 149.

[3] Parkman's *Jes. in North Am.* p. 436, note. Shea says that the Mascoutins disappeared from the Fox river region about 1720. *Wis. Hist. Col.*, vol. iii. p. 131 ; see also *Wis. Col.*, vol. iii. p. 106. Parkman says in his *La Salle*, p. 36, " The Mascoutins, Fire Nation, or Nation of the Prairie, are extinct or *merged in other tribes.*"

to the new abiding place of the Mascoutins,
should in some way, by more or less permanent occupation perhaps, have derived its
name from them is a reasonable supposition.
But whether Mascoutin mean fire nation or
prairie nation, it is now impossible absolutely
to determine. A feather's weight is thrown
into the balances in favor of the meaning fire
nation or fire land by Shea's statement that
Mashkooteaki means fire land ; for it will be
remembered that Radisson in his journal gives
the name Mascoutin as *Escotecke*—a not un-
successful phonetic reproduction of Mash-
kooteaki.[1]

The spot on Iowa soil now occupied by
Muscatine is not, it may fittingly be remarked
in conclusion, without other historic associations than such as arise from the probable
connection with it of some remnant of the
Mascoutin tribe.

[1] The following is suggested as the possible derivation of
the word Mascoutin: (1) Escotecke (Radisson) or Mash-
kooteaki (Shea) or Mashkootenki (Allouez and Marquette,
by prefixing *M*, and affixing *enk*, to the word *skoote* or *ash-
koote;* this word meaning, by definition of all, fire land or
fire nation); (2) Mashcouteng (*Jes. Rel.* 1669-70); (3)
Machkoutens (*Jes. Rel.* 1670-1); (4) Maskoutens or Mascoutins (Charlevoix). The meaning " prairie nation," to
which later writers have inclined, is obtained, according to
Shea, by deriving the word Mascoutin from Muskortenec or
Muscutah—" prairie."

Here was the favorite hunting-ground of the great Sac chief Makataimishckiakiak, or Black (sparrow) Hawk. Here, doubtless, on many occasions has he stood upon the commanding heights overlooking Mascoutin island and the Mississippi river, and gazed with awe upon the magnificent and extended prospect; for Black Hawk was an admirer of bold scenery, as he has been careful to tell us in his Autobiography when describing the position of and view from Black Hawk's Watch Tower on Rock river. Here also the eloquent and wily Sac chief Keokuk used to hunt and dwell; the name Keokuk lake still serving to designate an extension at one point of the waters of Muscatine slough. At Muscatine island Lieutenant Zebulon M. Pike, from whom was afterwards named Pike's Peak, Colorado, stopped on his voyage of exploration up the "great water"[1] in 1805. Up past Muscatine island sailed the expedition sent out in 1814 by Governor William Clark of Missouri to seize and fortify Prairie du Chien. Down past this island, likewise in 1814, swept the disabled boats of Lieutenants Rector and Riggs, after the bloody repulse at Rock island (by the Indians under Black Hawk) of Captain John

[1] Missi, Algonquin for great; sepe, Algonquin for water.

Campbell's expedition for the relief of the post at Prairie du Chien—then beleagured by the British. Down past this island the next year came in retreat, but not in disorder, the large boats in which Major Zachary Taylor had in vain, after some fierce cannonading, attempted to dislodge the British and Indians from their Rock Island stronghold. And finally, in 1816, up past Muscatine island and the future site of Muscatine, sailed General Thomas A. Smith of the American army, on his way to establish the military and trading post Fort Armstrong on the lower end of Rock Island, and the similar post, Fort Snelling, near the Falls of St. Anthony. No scene of blood, so far as known, ever has been enacted on the immediate spot where Muscatine stands. The most thrilling picture possible for the imagination to paint, in intimate connection with it, is that of a billowy mass of flames sweeping for miles the surface of a low, level island and bringing into sharp relief against the sky the form of some Indian watcher upon the lonely hills.

BLACK HAWK AND KEOKUK

BLACK HAWK, KEOKUK, AND THEIR VILLAGE.

THE western boundary of the state of Illinois is formed by the Mississippi river. The course of this river past the city of Rock Island, and for many miles above, is southwest. Just below the city Rock river enters the Mississippi. The course of Rock river is also southwest, but at such an angle as to bring it into conjunction with the larger stream at the point named. In the Mississippi, three and one-half miles northeast from the mouth of Rock river, is the island of Rock Island—at present the site of the extensive United States government works known as the Rock Island Arsenal. On the north bank of Rock river, a mile east from its mouth, was located for many years (perhaps a hundred) preceding its destruction in 1831 by the Illinois militia, the large Indian town of Saukenuk. The date of the founding of this town is undetermined. Black Hawk, the Sauk chief, in his autobiography, puts it as far back as 1731. Others put it as late as 1783—the approximate date of the abandonment by the

Sauks of their village on the Wisconsin river, which Augustin Grignon found deserted in 1795, but which Jonathan Carver, the English traveler, had found inhabited in 1766.

The founders of the town—the Sauk Indians—were an Algonquin tribe, inhabitants originally, along with other tribes, of the region about Montreal, Canada; extremely warlike in disposition, and possessing a history abounding in incidents both romantic and terrible. As early as 1720, according to Charlevoix, the pioneer historian of New France, they occupied the territory bordering upon Green Bay in what is now the State of Wisconsin; their village being on the Fox river thirty-seven miles above the bay, at the place afterwards called the little *Butte des Morts*. Here, it was one of their practices to demand tribute from the Indian traders as the latter passed up the Fox river on their way to the Wisconsin portage; pillaging, maltreating, and even killing any who should make bold to deny them. Enraged at this, a daring French trader and captain, LaPerriere Marin by name, resolved to put a stop to it. Waiting till the ice was sufficiently out of Fox river, in the spring of 1730, to permit the passage of boats, Capt. Marin ascended the stream with eight or ten Mackinaw craft filled with soldiers and Menomonee Indian allies. When within a mile of the Sauk village, he landed his boats, disembarked the Menomonees and half of his soldiers, and ordered them to gain the rear of the Sauks. The remainder of the party disposed themselves in the bottom of a few of the boats, beneath the canvas covers with which it was customary to protect the lading from the weather, and the expedition proceeded. As the boats came opposite the village, only Marin and the usual number of *voyageurs* were in sight. The shore was crowded with the dusky forms of the Indian warriors, women and children, who had gathered to receive the anticipated gift of goods and whiskey. Nothing could have been less sinister than the aspect of the boats. On they came, the clear tones of the *voyageurs* rising in the familiar boat song:

> "*Tous les printemps,*
> *Tant de nouvelles,*
> *Tous les amants*
> *Changent de maîtresses.*
> *Le bon vin m' endort;*
> *L' amour me réveille.*"[1]

[1] " Each returning springtime
Brings so much that's new,
All the fickle lovers
Changing sweethearts, too.
The good wine soothes and gives me rest,
While love inspires and fills my breast."

"Skootay wawbo! Skootay wawbo!" [fire water] yelled the Indians. "Fire!" cried Marin; and immediately the canvas coverings were thrown aside and the Indians smitten by a volley from more than a hundred rifles. Hearing the attack in front, the party which had been sent to cut off flight to the rear also attacked, and in a very short time the entire population of the village was destroyed, and the village itself reduced to ashes.[1] The mound afterwards raised above those who perished in the fight became known by the Anglo-French designation of the little *Butte des Morts.*

Prostrated by this and other disasters inflicted on their nation by the French,[2] the

[1] For the details of the above account of Marin's expedition the writer is indebted to a chapter from the " *Tales of the Northwest*," by William J. Snelling, Boston, 1830.

[2] The French war with the Sauk and Fox tribes was one of long duration. As early as 1716, the Sieur de Louvigny moved against them in their stronghold near Green Bay (Wis.) and forced them to sue for peace. In 1728, trouble again arose, and the Sieur de Lignery headed an expedition to Green Bay and up Fox river, which was rendered fruitless by the retreat of the Indians into the distant country of the Iowas. In the fall of 1729, a party of Ottawas, Chippeways, Menomonees, and Winnebagos (allies of the French) surprised the Foxes returning from a buffalo hunt, and killed eighty men and three hundred women and children. Next came Marin's expedition in March, 1730. In September, 1730, the Sieur de Villiers

Sauks—what there were left of them—sought out a new place of abode. They established a village on the present site of the twin villages, Prairie du Sac and Sauk City, on the Wisconsin river; their allies, the Foxes, who had suffered expulsion from the Green Bay country along with them, establishing themselves at Prairie du Chien. Writing concerning the Fox village at the Prairie, as it appeared in 1766, Jonathan Carver says:

"It is a large town and contains about three hundred families. The houses are well built, after the Indian manner, and pleasantly situated on a very rich soil from which they [the inhabitants] raise every necessary of life in great abundance. This town is the great mart, where all the adjacent tribes, and even those who inhabit the most remote branches of the Mississippi, annually assemble, about the latter end of May, bringing with them their furs to dispose of to the traders."

The town of Saukenuk was a much larger and much more important centre of Indian population than was Prairie du Chien. Its

defeated the Sauks and Foxes, killing two hundred warriors and six hundred women and children. 1746 is the date assigned by tradition for the final expulsion of the Sauks and Foxes from Wisconsin. But Carver distinctly bears testimony that both the Sauk and Fox tribes were inhabiting the country near the mouth of the Wisconsin river as late as 1766.

site was one of the most beautiful in the Mississippi valley. Northwest of it was the Mississippi, dotted with islands, foremost among which was Rock Island, abounding in fruits and birds, and presided over by a local divinity dwelling in a great cave at its northwest extremity. Immediately south and at one side of the town ran Rock river, a less imposing stream than the Father of Waters, but of silvery clearness, and broken by rippling shallows and gentle falls—a stream making always a pleasant noise in the ears of the dusky wanderers along its banks.

The general configuration of the town of Saukenuk was that of a right-angled triangle of unequal sides; the shorter side lying parallel with Rock river and extending down the river from the vertex of the right angle; the longer side extending north towards the Mississippi. It was defended by a brush palisade with gates for entrance. The lodges of the Indians were rectangular houses, from thirty to one hundred feet in length and from sixteen to forty feet in width. They were made by placing a covering or sheeting of elm bark over a framework of poles, the bark being fastened to the poles by buckskin thongs. A doorway, three feet in width by six in height, was left in the two ends of each lodge before which was usually suspended a skin of the buffalo. The interior was broken into compartments on either side of a hallway extending from end to end of the structure. At intervals, down the middle of this hallway, were fire pits, provision being made for the escape of the smoke from the fires by openings left in the roof directly over the pits. The compartments were used as sleeping rooms, the couch consisting of skins thrown over an elevated framework of elastic poles.[1] In nearly every detail of construction, these lodges of the Sauks at Saukenuk seem to have closely resembled those of the Hurons in Canada, which were swept out of existence over two hundred years ago, and our knowledge of which is only derived from the worm-eaten pages of the Jesuit Relations.[2]

Aside from warring with the Sioux, the chief occupation of the Sauks was agriculture. They cultivated some eight hundred acres of

[1] This description of Saukenuk is from the orally imparted recollections of Bailey Davenport, Esq., a son of Col. George Davenport. Mr. Bailey Davenport spent much of his childhood among the Indians at their village on Rock river. Col. George Davenport himself was an Indian trader residing on Rock Island. The son was born in September, 1823, and died in January, 1891.

[2] Parkman in "*The Jesuits in North America*" (Introduction, pp. xxvi and xxvii), describes particularly the lodges of the Hurons.

the land adjacent to their village, raising good crops of corn, beans, and pumpkins. For an Indian town, the population of Saukenuk was very large. Governor Ford, in his history of Illinois, estimates it at six or seven thousand persons. Other estimates put it at not less than ten thousand persons. Major Thomas Forsyth, of the United States army, wrote to Governor Clark, of Missouri, in 1817: "Indeed I have seen many Indian villages, but I never saw such a large one or such a populous one. They (the Sauks) appear stationary there, and their old lodges are repaired, and some new ones built and others building." Here, in this savage London or Paris, was the centre of the Sauk national life, of its gaieties and of its serious deliberations.

On the level ground west of the town frequently might have been seen, in the early summer time and autumn, hundreds of brawny Indians engaged in their favorite sports of horse racing and ball playing. In either case the play was for stakes, and these always high —two or three horses, a fine rifle or war club. Their game of ball, which Black Hawk mentions as very popular, was played in this wise: A tall post was erected at either extremity of the play ground, and the players divided into

rival parties. The object of each was to de-
fend its own post and drive the ball to that
of its adversary. "Hundreds of lithe and
agile figures," says Parkman, describing this
game as played by the Sauks and Ojibways
near Michillimackinac in June, 1763, "are
leaping and bounding upon the plain; each
is nearly naked, his loose black hair flying in
the wind; and each bears in his hand a bat
of a form peculiar to this game. At one
moment the whole are crowded together, a
dense throng of combatants, all struggling
for the ball; at the next they are scattered
again, and running over the ground like
hounds in full cry; each in his excitement
yells and shouts at the height of his voice.
Rushing and striking, tripping their adversa-
ries or hurling them to the ground, they pur-
sue the animating contest." Or, if our at-
tention be directed to the town itself on the
proper occasion, we may behold the great
national dance of the Sauks. The large open
square with which the town is provided is
swept clean. The chiefs and old warriors take
seats on mats which have been spread on the
upper end of the square. Next come the
drummers and singers; the braves and women gather on the sides. The drums beat
and the singing commences. A warrior en-

ters the square, keeping time to the music.
He describes the way in which a war party
was formed, the enemy approached, the toma-
hawk buried in the brain of a· victim, or his
scalp torn from his head.   The women loudly
applaud, while the young men who have never
killed any enemy stand back ashamed.   Another warrior then steps forward and recounts
his exploits, until all have done so, and a veri-
table frenzy of excitement seizes upon the
assembly.

At a distance of half a mile east of the site
of the Indian town rises the bold promontory
known as Black Hawk's Watch-Tower.   Rock
river flows at its base,—two hundred sheer
feet from the apex in which the promontory
culminates.   Of this place Black Hawk himself says in his autobiography: "This tower,
to which my name has been applied, was a
favorite resort, and was frequently visited by
me alone, where I could sit and smoke my
pipe and look with wonder and pleasure at
the grand scenes that were presented by the
sun's rays even across the mighty water [the
Mississippi].   On one occasion a Frenchman,
who had been making his home in our village,
brought his violin with him to the tower to
play and dance for the amusement of our
people who had assembled there, and while

dancing with his back to the cliff, accidentally fell over and was killed by the fall. The Indians say that always, at the same time of the year, soft strains of the violin can be heard near the spot."

The two most remarkable individuals (and they were truly remarkable) at any time born in Saukenuk were Black Hawk and Keokuk, both war chiefs of the Sauks. The date of the birth of Black Hawk or, as the name is in the Sauk tongue, Makataimeshekiakiak, is given in the autobiography as 1767. If this date be accepted, the conclusion is inevitable that the Sauks must have removed from the Wisconsin to the Rock river region immediately after the visit to them of Carver in 1766. But there are those who, governed by statements made by Black Hawk some years after the publication of his autobiography, fix the date of his birth as 1775. This later date approximates that already named (1783) as the possible time at which Saukenuk was founded.

In respect to personal character, Black Hawk was a man of marked strength and nobility. A savage by birth, he yet was singularly without the instincts of the savage. Although polygamy was practiced by his people, he never had but one wife. He realized the

peculiarly demoralizing effect of intoxicants
upon the Indian, and rarely, if ever, could be
induced to depart from his rule of abstinence.
He respected the helpless women and children of an enemy, and showed clemency even
to male captives. A striking instance of his
clemency to such a captive, is related by the
scout, Elijah Kilbourn. In the war of 1812,
Kilbourn was attached to the American army.
Black Hawk and a band of Sauk warriors were
serving in the ranks of the British. After the
repulse of the British and Indians at Fort
Stephenson in August, 1813, Black Hawk became disgusted with the ill fortune just then
attending the British arms and took summary
leave for Rock river. Kilbourn with a party
was sent by the Americans to follow him.
The pursuit was continued until the party, becoming confused by many trails, and being in
the midst of Indian settlements, was forced to
break up, each man looking out for his own
safety. Suddenly, one day, on emerging from
a thicket, Kilbourn saw at a distance an Indian on his hands and knees slaking his thirst
at a spring. Instinctively the scout leveled
his rifle and pulled the trigger. The flint was
shivered against the pan, but the priming
failed to ignite. By this time the Indian had
recovered himself and was leveling his rifle at

the scout.   He did not fire, however, but advanced upon Kilbourn and made him prisoner.
Being ordered to march ahead of his captor,
Kilbourn soon found himself in an Indian
camp.   Here, gaining a closer look, he
recognized his captor as none other than
Black Hawk himself.   "The white mole digs
deep, but Makataimeshekiakiak flies high and
can see far off," said Black Hawk to the scout.
After some words to his band, Black Hawk
informed Kilbourn that he had decided to
adopt him into the Sauk tribe.   Accordingly,
he was taken to Saukenuk, dressed and painted
and formally received into the Sauk fellowship.   Constantly watchful for a chance to
escape, at length, after three years, he found
it and regained civilization.   But this was not
all—nor, had it been all, would it perhaps have
been so very remarkable; for an Indian not in-
frequently has been known to spare a captive,
through caprice, and adopt him as a brother.
What followed Kilbourn's escape, however, is
remarkable.   During the Black Hawk war of
1832, he was again a scout in the service of
the government, and was captured by Black
Hawk at the battle (so called) of Stillman's
Run.   He nerved himself for the torture which
he felt certain must now await him.   Nor was
he reassured in the least when Black Hawk,

passing close to him, said in a low tone, "Does the mole think that Black Hawk forgets?" But, just before sunset of the day of his capture, Black Hawk again came to him, loosed the cords that bound him to a tree and conducted him far into the forest. Pausing, the Indian said, "I am going to send you back to your chief, though I ought to kill you for running away a long time ago, after I had adopted you as a son; but Black Hawk can forgive as well as fight."[1]

The cause of Black Hawk's friendship for the British, as against the Americans, is plain; the British were careful to keep their engagements with the Indians, while the Americans were not. The British Indian department was filled by men of long experience in Indian affairs, and proved a most potent instrumentality for enlisting the Indians on the side of the British whenever occasion required. In contrast to this, the American Indian department was largely in the hands of men who had never seen an Indian until they met him in the difficult and delicate relations of Indian agent. When, therefore, on the breaking out of the war of 1812, Col. Robert Dickson,

[1] Kilbourn's narrative may be found, reprinted from "*The Soldier's Cabinet*," in Patterson's second edition of *Black Hawk's Autobiography*. The main points are also given by Black Hawk himself. Autobiog. 2d ed. pp. 37, 98.

of the British Indian department sent word
to the Sauks at Rock river to meet him at
Green Bay, preparatory to moving against the
Americans, they complied with alacrity. Black
Hawk personally participated in the fight at
the River Raisen, near Malden, on January
22d, 1813, where he interposed to keep his
warriors from joining in the massacre of
American prisoners which was going on.
Later, on May 5th, he was at the siege of Fort
Meigs; and finally, on August 2d, took a
hand in the attack on Fort Stephenson. Many
years ago, a writer in the Baltimore *American*,
to whose credibility the editor of the paper
bore testimony, stated that Black Hawk had
told him that he also had fought in the battle
of the Thames. "During a residence of several years in what is now the territory of Iowa,"
says the writer, " I had many opportunities of
seeing and conversing with Black Hawk. . . .
In the course of our talk, I asked him if he
was with Tecumseh when he was killed. 'I
was,' said Black Hawk, 'and I will now tell
you all about it.'" Then follows a circum-
stantial narrative of the battle, ending in these
words:

"At the first discharge of their [the Americans']
guns, I saw Tecumseh stagger forwards over a
fallen tree near which he was standing, letting his

rifle drop at his feet. As soon as the Indians discovered he was killed, a panic came over them, and, fearing that the Great Spirit was displeased, they fought no longer."

Besides the foregoing, W. Henry Starr, Esq., of Burlington, Iowa Territory, wrote as follows, on March 21st, 1839:

"In the autumn of 1838, Black Hawk was at the house of an Indian trader in the vicinity of Burlington, when I became acquainted, and frequently conversed with him in broken English, and through the medium of gestures and pantomime. . . . On one occasion, I mentioned Tecumseh to him, and he expressed the greatest joy that I had heard of him; and, pointing away to the east and making a feint as if aiming a gun, said: 'Chemokaman [white man] nesso [kill]'; from which I have no doubt of his being personally acquainted with Tecumseh; and I have been since informed, on good authority, that he was in the battle of the Thames and in several other engagements with that distinguished chief."

These would seem to be strong evidences that Black Hawk did not sever his connection with the British army until October, 1813, when the battle of the Thames was fought. Nevertheless, in the autobiography, it is explicitly stated by Black Hawk that he and twenty of his warriors quietly left the British camp immediately after the repulse at Fort

Stephenson.   If this were not the fact, it is hard to understand why it is stated so to be in the autobiography, which in essentials is a trustworthy recital.

The occurrence which caused the name of Black Hawk to become universally known in America, was the Black Hawk War of 1832.[1] This wretched contest was the outgrowth of misunderstanding and of the encroachment of white settlers upon the public domain.   In 1804, at St. Louis, William Henry Harrison negotiated with several chiefs of the Sauk and Fox tribes a treaty, whereby were ceded to the United States many thousand acres of lands in Wisconsin and Illinois, including the site of Saukenuk.   The validity of this treaty was never recognized by Black Hawk.   He contended that the chiefs who signed it had no authority to do so, and, moreover, that they were induced to affix their names by grossly unfair means.   However this may have been, the Indians by the terms of the

[1] The Black Hawk War is more justly famous for the many men participating in it who afterwards gained distinction in both the military and civil walks than for anything else.   Among them were Abraham Lincoln, Jefferson Davis, Zachary Taylor, Albert Sidney Johnston, Robert Anderson, of Fort Sumter celebrity, Phil Kearney and W. S. Harney, besides three governors of Illinois, — Ford, Duncan and Reynolds.

treaty were permitted to occupy the ceded lands until such time as they should be sold to settlers; and when, before they were thus sold, settlers began to locate in the vicinity of Saukenuk, difficulties between the Indians and these settlers naturally arose.   Finally, in 1831, the exasperation on both sides became intense, and an appeal was made by the settlers to Governor Reynolds, of Illinois, and to General Gaines, of the United States army, at Jefferson Barracks, Mo., forthwith to remove the Indians from the State.   Governor Reynolds thereupon called out the militia, and General Gaines started for Fort Armstrong, Rock Island, arriving there on June 3d with six companies of regulars.   Black Hawk was summoned to a conference by General Gaines, which he and his braves attended, decked out in their war paint and bearing their war clubs. To the general's order to move across the river into the Iowa country, he returned a stubborn refusal.   Later in the month, the militia ascended Rock river in a steamboat to Vandruff's Island, which they found deserted, as also the Indian town below it. Black Hawk and his band had quietly removed across the Mississippi.   But the militia, feeling it necessary to expend their martial ardor upon something, set fire to the ancient

metropolis of the Sauks and watched it con-
sume to ashes.

On June 30th, a formal engagement was entered into, between Black Hawk and General
Gaines and Governor Reynolds, that the Sauk
and Fox nations should at all times thereafter
reside and hunt on the west side of the Mississippi river, and not return to the east side
without the express consent of the president
of the United States or of the governor of
Illinois. This engagement Black Hawk failed
to keep. Just what actuated him most in
breaking it perhaps is not clear, but among
the motives at work stand out prominently an
unconquerable love for the place of his birth
and a desire there to spend the declining
years of his life. Viewed from his standpoint,
the Rock river country had never rightfully
passed from the control of the Sauks; it was
the scene of the chief events in the life of that
nation since their expulsion from Wisconsin; nature, moreover, had made it very beautiful. In returning to it, to reclaim it, if
possible,—that is, if the Winnebagoes and
the Pottawattomies should join him, and the
British render efficient aid, as he believed
they would,—Black Hawk showed himself
inspired in no small degree by the same
spirit of patriotism that in ancient days made

a hero of Epaminondas, and in modern of Washington.

The re-appearance of the Sauks on Rock river, it is needless to say, produced a great commotion. Again the militia were called out, and the regulars, this time under command of General Atkinson, reinforced Fort Armstrong. Many murders were committed by Indians in different parts of Illinois ; almost all of them, however, by the Winnebagoes,—none by Black Hawk's band. But there were no considerable accessions to the invading force, which at the start numbered only about two hundred partially armed braves and warriors. Beginning at length to realize the futility of the attempt he was making, Black Hawk sent a flag of truce to Major Stillman, who was in command of the advance guard of the militia, and who with his men was at this time (May 15th, 1832) encamped near a small stream since every-where known as Stillman's Run. The bearers of this flag were taken into custody by some of Stillman's men, and soon after a general rush was made by the whole command upon a small party of Black Hawk's warriors that was descried in the distance. Having succeeded in killing two of these, the militiamen pushed forward till, falling into an ambuscade hastily set for them by Black Hawk himself, they were put to wild and ignominious flight. The story is told by Governor Ford, in his History of Illinois, that in Stillman's command was a member of the legal profession just returned from riding the circuit. He had with him a pair of saddle-bags containing a change of under-garments and several law books. These fell into the hands of the Indians, and the learned barrister used to relate with much vexation that Black Hawk "had decked himself out in his finery, appearing in the wild woods, amongst his savage companions, dressed in a ruffled shirt drawn over his deer-skin leggins, with a volume of 'Chitty's Pleadings' under each arm."

The fight at Stillman's Run was followed by others, notably those of Peckatonica Creek and Wisconsin Heights, both very disastrous to the Indians; until, finally, their whole force was scattered, killed or captured at the battle of Bad Axe. Black Hawk, together with his old friend Winneshiek, the prophet, fled to the Big Dells, Wisconsin, where in August, 1832, he was discovered by the Winnebago chiefs, Chaeter and the One-Eyed De Caury, and taken to General Street at Prairie du Chien. From Prairie du Chien, he was sent to Jefferson Barracks, Missouri. After some months spent there in confinement, he was taken east, with a number of other Indians (among them Keokuk), and shown the great cities and wonderful resources of the American people. He made a second visit to the east in 1837, and died in October, 1838, at his lodge on the Iowa river, near Iowaville, to which locality he had removed shortly after his return from his first visit to the east.

It was just after this first eastern visit that Black Hawk prepared and dictated his autobiography—by far his greatest achievement of any kind, and destined to make not merely his name, but his thoughts and his feelings, known to distant times. It reveals him as possessed of lofty instincts; a man of action, but still more a man of observation and reflection; a savage rising superior to the plane of savage existence, yet illustrating and illuminating the ways of civilization by bringing them to the test of primitive standards. Moreover, it is thoroughly unique—the only true autobiography of an Indian extant. The manner of its production and publication is interesting. Black Hawk, having conceived the idea of putting in writing the reasons for his course in returning to Rock river, after the expulsion of his tribe in 1831, made it known to Antoine Le Claire, the United States

Indian interpreter at Rock Island. Le Claire engaged a young printer, J. B. Patterson by name, as amanuensis, and the task was begun; —Black Hawk dictating to Le Claire, Le Claire translating to Patterson, and Patterson committing to paper. After the whole was finished, Le Claire carefully read it all over to Black Hawk, to make sure of its accuracy. It was then officially certified to by Le Claire and printed by Patterson, the original edition being in small, crude volumes bound in covers of common paste-board. Le Claire was until 1861, when he died, a highly respected resident of Davenport, Iowa, and Patterson in the last year (1891) has died, at an advanced age, in Oquawka, Illinois, where he has long lived and where he ever has been known as a man of the strictest honor. There can, therefore, be no doubt of the authenticity of the record which these men were the means of placing before the public. Besides, the internal evidence of authenticity is convincing. William J. Snelling (a son of Colonel Josiah Snelling of the United States Army, after whom Fort Snelling, Minnesota, was named), says in the *North American Review* for January, 1835:

"That this [Black Hawk's Autobiography] is the *bona fide* work of Black Hawk, we have the respectable testimony of Antoine Le Claire, the government interpreter for the Sacs and Foxes, and what (as we have not the honor of being acquainted with that gentleman) we deem more conclusive, the intrinsic evidence of the work itself. We will venture to affirm (and having long dwelt among the aborigines, we conceive ourselves entitled to do so) that no one but a Sac Indian could have written or dictated such a composition. No white man, however great his ability may be, could have executed a work so thoroughly and truly Indian."

In the autobiography, Black Hawk expresses opinions upon many subjects,—among them, marriage, land ownership, rotation in office, the savage, as contrasted with the civilized, mode of warfare, the American Indian establishment, the colonization of the negroes. As to land ownership, he was a precursor of Henry George, saying :

"My reason teaches me that land cannot be sold. The Great Spirit gave it to his children to live upon and cultivate, as far as necessary for their subsistence, and so long as they occupy and cultivate it they have a right to the soil, but if they voluntarily leave it then any other people have a right to settle on it. Nothing can be sold but such things as can be carried away."

His conclusion on politics, as he had seen the game manipulated, was that—

"The white people seem never to be satisfied. When they get a good father, they hold councils at the suggestion of some bad, ambitious man, who wants the place himself, and conclude among themselves that this man, or some other equally ambitious, would make a better father than they have, and nine times out of ten they don't get as good a one again."

"He would recommend," he said, "to his Great Father [the President] the propriety of breaking up the present Indian establishment (under which new and inexperienced men were constantly sent to deal with the Indians) and creating a new one; making the commanding officers at the different frontier posts the agents of the government for the different nations of Indians."

In this recommendation, which is quite as *apropos* to-day as when made by Black Hawk in 1833, most disinterested persons will heartily concur. On the then absorbing question of negro slavery, his views were unique.

"I find," he says, "that a number of states admit no slaves, whilst the remainder hold the negroes as slaves and are anxious, but do not know how, to get clear of them. I will now give my plan, which when understood I hope will be adopted. Let the free states remove all the negroes within their limits to the slave states; then let our Great Father buy all the female negroes in the slave states between the ages of twelve and · twenty, and sell them to the people of the free

states for a term of years,—say, those under fifteen until they are twenty-one, and those of and
over fifteen for five years ; and continue to buy
all the females in the slave states as soon as they
arrive at the age of twelve, and take them to the
free states and dispose of them in the same way
as the first ; and it will not be long before the
country is clear of the black skins, about whom,
I am told, they have been talking for a long time,
and for whom they have expended a large amount
of money. I have no doubt but our Great Father
would do his part in accomplishing this object
for his children, as he could not lose much by it,
and would make them all happy. If the free
states did not want them all for servants, we would
take the remainder in our nation to help our
women make corn."

When in New York, he had witnessed a
balloon ascension, and, concerning this,
remarks:

"We had seen many wonderful sights . . . .
large villages, the great national road over the
mountains, the railroad, steam carriages, ships,
steamboats, and many other things ; but we were
now about to witness a sight more surprising than
any of these. We were told that a man was going up in the air in a balloon. We watched with
anxiety to see if this could be true ; and, to our
utter astonishment, saw him ascend in the air until the eye could no longer perceive him. Our
people were all surprised, and one of our young

men asked the prophet [Winneshiek] if he was going up to see the Great Spirit."

He and his party were also treated to a display of fire-works at Castle Garden, on which he makes the shrewd yet characteristically Indian comment that "it was an agreeable entertainment, but to the whites who witnessed it less magnificent than would have been the sight of one of our large prairies when on fire." The American women whom he met treated him handsomely, giving him small presents, and he condescends to say of them that they were "very kind, very good, and very pretty—for pale faces."

Black Hawk's defense of his course in the Black Hawk war constitutes the principal part of his autobiography, and is plausible,—in many respects just. The line of it already has been intimated, however, and more is not necessary here.

Next to Black Hawk, Keokuk is the leading figure among the Sauks. He was younger than Black Hawk, having been born about 1788, and was descended, on his mother's side, it is said, from the noted Captain Marin.[1] He was a fine athlete and horseman, and extremely vain. Inferior to the older chief in

[1] *Recollections of Augustin Grignon*, vol. III, p. 211, Wis. Hist. Soc. Col.

simplicity and dignity of character, he was
far superior to him in wit, tact and shrewd-
ness.   Early perceiving the folly of contending against the power and resources of the
whites, he so shaped his course as to gain the
white man's favor.   When word came that
the Sauks must remove from the Rock river,
he promptly obeyed and sought a new abode
on the Iowa.   For his compliance in this
thing and in others, he was recognized by the
United States government as head chief of
his nation, a proceeding which gave mortal
offense to Black Hawk.

Of Keokuk's wit a striking instance has
been preserved.   It seems (so the story runs)
that on one occasion after the removal of the
Sauks west of the Mississippi, they were summoned to a conference with the Mormons at
Nauvoo, Illinois, by Joe Smith, the Mormon
prophet.   The object of the wily prophet in
seeking the conference was to persuade the
Indians into relinquishing to him certain
lands which he coveted for the church.   He
accordingly prepared with great care the plea
which he should make to them.   At the appointed time, Keokuk and the prophet, each
in his best attire and attended by an imposing
retinue, met in the Mormon temple.   In concluding his address, the prophet said that it

had been divinely communicated to him that
the Indian tribes of North America were the
lost tribes of the House of Israel.   Moreover,
he had been commissioned from on high to
assemble such of them as were near him and
to remove them from where they were to a
new land—a land flowing with milk and
honey.   To this Keokuk listened very atten-
tively, and, after a respectful interval, he rose
with much dignity to reply.   As to whether
or not the American Indians were the lost
tribes spoken of by the prophet, he said he
would not attempt to determine.   This, however, he would say: of milk his people were
not fond—they much preferred water; and
as for honey, it was to be had in ample quan-
tities in the land they then occupied.   Could
not the prophet enter more fully into particulars ?   Did the government, in this land
to which he desired the Indians to move, pay
large annuities ? and was there there a plen-
tiful supply of whiskey?   The conference, it
need hardly be told, came to an abrupt termination.[1]

Keokuk's most remarkable gift was his eloquence.   This, according to all contemporary
accounts, was in the highest degree stirring
and effective.   It brought him into great

[1] *Recollections of Uriah Briggs.* Annals of Iowa, 1865.

prominence both among the Indians and in councils between them and the Americans. When Black Hawk was inciting Keokuk's band to return with him to Illinois and join his own braves in the struggle they were about to make to re-possess the ancient home of the Sauks, the eloquence and address of Keokuk were put to a severe test. He knew that the attempt must end in disaster, but the passions of his followers were aroused and were difficult to allay. His first words to them, therefore, were of sympathy with their alleged wrongs. He told them that they had been unjustly treated, and hence were entitled to revenge. He even offered to lead them against their foe, "but," said he,

"upon this condition : that we first put our wives and children and our aged men gently to sleep in that slumber which knows no waking this side the spirit land, ... for we go upon the long trail which has no turn."

At the conclusion of his address, the desire of his young men for war was considerably abated.

After the surrender of Black Hawk in August, 1832, a treaty was entered into between the Sauks and the United States, whereby the latter acquired the whole of eastern Iowa. This treaty, on the part of the United States, was negotiated by Gen. Winfield Scott, and, at the request of the Indians, provided

"that there should be granted to Antoine Le Claire, interpreter, a part Indian, one section of land opposite Rock Island,[1] and one section at the head of the first rapids above said island, within the county ceded by the Sauks and Foxes."

At the negotiation of the treaty, Keokuk was the principal speaker on the part of the Indians. His death occurred in the State of Kansas, whither the remnant of his tribe ultimately removed. It was comparatively ignoble, being the result of too heavy potations.

Incidentally, mention already has been made of the island of Rock Island, which is situated in the Mississippi river, not far from the site once occupied by Saukenuk. This island is noteworthy on two accounts: its natural beauty and its romantic history. Its extreme length is two and seven-eighths miles, and its extreme width four-fifths of a mile. Its area is eight hundred acres, and originally it was covered by a dense growth of the oak, black walnut, elm, and basswood. Its substructure is rock, and it stands twenty feet above the highest freshets. In the eyes of the Indians, it was not only a spot of sur-

[1] Now the site of a part of the city of Davenport, Iowa.

passing loveliness, but was invested with a certain sacred charm.   Says Black Hawk :

"It was our garden, like the white people have near their big villages, which supplied us with strawberries, blackberries, gooseberries, plums, apples, and nuts of different kinds. Being situated at the foot of the rapids, its waters supplied us with the finest fish. In my early life, I spent many happy days on this island. A good spirit had charge of it, which lived in a cave in the rocks immediately under the place where the fort now stands. This guardian spirit has often been seen by our people. It was white, with large wings like a swan's, but ten times larger. We were particular not to make much noise in that part of the island which it inhabited, for fear of disturbing it. But the noise at the fort has since driven it away, and no doubt a bad spirit has taken its place."

Rock Island made its first considerable appearance in history as far back as 1812. At that time the whole Northwest was practically a dense wilderness. There were trading settlements of log huts and wigwams at Detroit and Michillimackinac, in what is now the state of Michigan, and at Green Bay, Prairie du Chien, and Milwaukee, in what is now the state of Wisconsin. Fort Madison had been built and abandoned within the present limits of Iowa, and a few primitive abodes marked the site of Chicago, Illinois. On the lower Mississippi were the old French posts, Kaskaskia, Cahokia, and St. Louis. The inhabitants of these various places were fur traders and Canadian *voyageurs*, the latter a most interesting and picturesque class, improvident and light-hearted to a degree, spending the winter in hard labor, on a diet of corn and tallow, and lounging through the summer. Among the traders was a very remarkable man—one who exerted the greatest influence over the Sauk and Fox tribes. This man was Colonel Robert Dickson. He was an Englishman, who had come to America in 1790 to traffic with the Indians, sacrificing to this end a good social connection and the comforts of civilization.

In the Spring of 1814, Governor William Clark of Missouri sent an expedition to take possession of Prairie du Chien and erect a fort there. The fort was placed on a small elevation back of the settlement, mounted with six cannon and garrisoned by a force of seventy men under Lieutenant Joseph Perkins. It was named Fort Shelby. Suddenly, on July 17th, there appeared before it a motley force of British traders' clerks and Indians, six hundred and fifty in all, from Michillimackinac, under Lieutenant Colonel William

McKay; and, after a spirited interchange of
cannon balls, the fort capitulated. Meanwhile, under the direction of General Benjamin Howard, of the United States army, an
expedition was fitting out at St. Louis to rein-
force the garrison at Fort Shelby. This
expedition, consisting of three barges carrying a force of regular troops and rangers,
under the command of Captain John Campbell, of the First United States Infantry, started
for Prairie du Chien on July 18th, ignorant,
of course, of the fact that Fort Shelby had
capitulated the day before. All went well
until Rock Island was reached. Here the
boats cast anchor for the night. The Indians
swarmed about them in great numbers, making loud professions of friendship, but quietly
signifying to the French boatmen in charge
that they desired them to abandon their
American comrades and return down the
river. This the Indians did by seizing the
hands of the Frenchmen and gently pulling
them in a down stream direction. It was
evident that the Indians meant to attack
the boats, but did not wish to injure their
old-time friends, the French.[1] The danger

[1] Black Hawk explains in the Autobiography that the
Indians were at first sincere in their expressions of friendship for the Americans on this occasion, but that during the

was made known to Campbell, but he discredited its existence. The next morning the fleet set sail without hindrance, Campbell being in immediate command of the boat containing the regulars, and Captain Stephen Rector and Lieutenant Riggs, respectively, of the other two. The wind had risen and become so fierce that, just above Rock Island, Campbell's boat was driven on a large island near the mainland, ever since known as Campbell's Island. Sentinels were placed, and the men debarked and began cooking their breakfast. But in a moment the Indians, in hundreds, were upon them, delivering a deadly fire. Many were killed and wounded. Those who were unharmed took refuge in the boat. Among the wounded was Campbell himself. To add to the peril of the situation, the boat took fire. Black Hawk, who commanded the Indians in the attack, explains that this was due to fire arrows prepared by himself and shot by him against the sail.

In the meantime, the other two barges, which had drawn far ahead of that commanded by Campbell, had, with the greatest

night word reached them of the capture of Fort Shelby by the British, and that the British desired them to join in the war against the Americans. This they could not find it in their hearts to refuse to do.

difficulty, succeeded in returning to his aid.
Rector's men, who were good sailors, first
lightened their boat by casting overboard a
large quantity of provisions, and then, leaping into the water on the side furthest from
the Indians, pushed it broadside on against
the burning boat of Campbell. The unharmed and the wounded were quickly trans-
ferred to Rector's boat, which, having been
got back into the stream, was rowed night and
day until it reached St. Louis. The boat of
Riggs was outwardly in the possession of the
Indians for some hours, but, it being well
fortified, the Indians were unable to injure
those within, and finally withdrew. It then
followed Rector's boat down the river.

The rough handling which Campbell's expedition had received at the hands of the
Sauk and Fox tribes naturally excited much
resentment at St. Louis, and early in September an expedition was started for their villages to chastise them, and also to establish a
fort on Rock Island. In this instance, the
expedition consisted of three hundred and
thirty-four officers and men, in several large
barges armed with cannon, and was in command of Major Zachary Taylor, of the regular service. But the Indians had kept the
British at Fort Shelby (now Fort McKay)

informed of the approach of the Americans,
and a warm reception had been prepared for
them.   Captain Thos. G. Anderson, to whom
the command of the fort had been turned
over after its capture, had sent down to Rock
Island a detachment of thirty men with three
pieces of artillery.   The artillery had been
planted on the west side of the island near
the foot of the rapids, it being supposed that
Taylor's expedition was for the recapture of
the fort at Prairie du Chien, and, therefore,
must pass up the narrow channel between the
island and what is now the Iowa shore.   But
when the boats came to anchor (as they did
by stress of the wind) some distance below
the foot of Rock Island, the guns had to be
dragged to a position further down stream.
This, however, was successfully accomplished,
and on the morning of September 6, 1814, a
brisk and well directed fire was opened, which
after a short time so riddled the barges that
they were obliged to drop down stream out
of range.   A council of war was then called
by Taylor, and it being the unanimous opin-
ion that the enemy was too strong to be
overcome by the force at hand, the whole
expedition set sail for Fort Madison, where it
landed, and where Major Taylor wrote to
General Howard his official report of what

had transpired.   It was the least glorious contest in which the future hero of Buena Vista
and Monterey was destined to be engaged.

Finally, nearly two years after the conclusion of peace with Great Britain, the United
States government was able to place Rock
Island under military control.   In May, 1816,
General Thos. A. Smith landed at the island
without opposition, left the 8th United States
Infantry, under Colonel Lawrence, with orders to erect a fort ; while he himself pushed
on to establish a post (now Fort Snelling)
near the Falls of St. Anthony.   Selecting the
extreme northwest point of the island, Colonel
Lawrence laid off a rectangular space, four
hundred feet each way, and surrounded it by
walls of hewn timber resting upon a substructure of stone.   At the northeast, southeast,
and southwest angles, he caused block houses
to be built, and these he provided with cannon.
On the interior, against one side of the square,
were erected the soldiers' barracks.   They
were of hewn timber, the roofs being made to
slope inward, that it might be difficult for the
Indians to set them on fire.   When completed, the work was christened Fort Armstrong, in honor of the then Secretary of War.
Coming suddenly into the view of the lonely
voyager up the Mississippi, its whitewashed

walls and towers appeared, it has been said, not unlike the outworks of one of "those enchanted castles in an uninhabited desert so well described in the Arabian Nights Entertainments."

Fort Armstrong (long since demolished) was never subjected to the ordeal of an Indian attack, but only narrowly escaped it on two occasions. The first was not long after its erection. One day, while most of the men were at some distance from the walls felling trees, a party of warriors headed by Chief Nekalequot, landed on the north side of the island and asked permission to dance in front of the commandant's headquarters. About the same time, another party of warriors, headed by Keokuk, was discovered approaching the fort from the south side of the island. Suspecting treachery, the Colonel immediately had the recall sounded for the men and the cannon run out. The Indians were then ordered to disperse, which they did with some precipitation.

With Colonel Lawrence, there came to Rock Island, as contractor for supplies to the post, a very striking character — Colonel George Davenport. Colonel Davenport was a native of England, had been first a sailor and then a soldier, in the latter capacity having served on the American side in the war of 1812. He built a house on the island

near the fort, and engaged in trade with the
Indians.   In time he became very popular
with them, and was freely consulted by them.
Black Hawk especially reposed great confidence in him, and makes frequent reference
to him in the autobiography.   It perhaps
was due to his presence on the island that
the second projected attack upon the fort was
not made.   Be that as it may, in April, 1832,
Black Hawk, having recrossed the Mississippi
to the Illinois shore, came up opposite the
island with his two hundred warriors at early
evening, and, after meditatively surveying it
for some time, crossed to it at one of the
fords.   The fort was feebly garrisoned at the
time, and crowded with panic-stricken settlers; as also was the stockade with which
Colonel Davenport had surrounded the log
store and dwelling built by him in 1818, one-
half mile northeast of the fort.   But the Indians did nothing, and by dawn a steamboat
had arrived from Jefferson Barracks, bringing
a reinforcement to the fort.   On July 4, 1845,
Colonel Davenport was murdered in his
house (a later and more pretentious structure
than that of 1818) by a band of outlaws, during the absence of his family at a picnic gathering.   The object of the miscreants was money,
but they got little.   Since then this house

has been abandoned, and now stands a pictur-esque ruin on the banks of the Mississippi.

With the incident last related, the history of Rock Island ceases to be romantic. In 1862, the United States government passed an act establishing there a national arsenal. The work was begun by General Rodman, and was continued under his able successor, General D. W. Flagler. Ten immense shops of stone have been erected, and when all is completed, it is estimated that from this arse-nal alone can be armed, equipped, and sup-plied an army of 750,000 men. Nor have the æsthetic possibilities of the island been lost sight of. It is still, as it was in the days of Black Hawk, a charmed spot. Its wood-land has been left largely intact, and the phebe, the oriole, the cuckoo, and a host of other birds flit among the branches; while beneath, from one's too intrusive feet, scud away the pheasant, the rabbit, and the squir-rel. It is intersected by quiet and secluded drives and walks, and abounds in dim loiter-ing places. But its greatest charm is that with which it forever has been invested by the words and deeds of the noted chieftain, now, like Hiawatha, departed

"To the Islands of the Blessed,
  To the land of the Hereafter."

NAUVOO AND THE PROPHET

NAUVOO AND THE PROPHET.

"A church without a prophet is not the church for me."
Mormon Hymn.

INTRODUCTORY.

THE reformed branch of the Mormon church, or church of Jesus Christ of Latter-day Saints, comprises in Iowa some six thousand persons, and in the world not far from thirty thousand. Its headquarters now are at the village of Lamoni, Iowa, in Decatur county. Here it owns a church building containing a large auditorium and such other rooms as convenience requires. Besides this building, the society owns in Lamoni a substantial publishing house whence are issued the Holy Scriptures, (a translation and revision of the old and new Testaments by Joseph the Prophet) the golden Bible or Book of Mormon, the Book of doctrine and covenants, the Life of Joseph the Prophet by Tullige, and another life of Joseph by his mother, entitled Joseph Smith and his Progenitors. This branch of the Mormon church eschews polygamy and

the doctrine of a blood atonement.[1] It claims
to adhere strictly to the teachings of Joseph
the prophet as contained in the Book of Mormon. At its head is Joseph Smith, Jr., son
of the founder of the Mormon faith—a man
of exemplary life and character and of entire
sincerity. Proselytes to the society are made
by missionaries, who are sent to England, to
Wales, to Denmark, to Australia, and to the
Society Islands. Some also are won to its
membership through a mission which is main-
tained in Utah.

The events which led to the establishment
of the reformed Mormon church may briefly
be told. On the Exodus of the Mormons
from Nauvoo in 1846, Joseph Smith, son of
the prophet, remained behind with Emma
Smith, his mother. Intimidation and violence
were made use of by Brigham Young to com-
pel Emma Smith to follow the fortunes of the
church, but without avail. Indeed, the evidence
is strong that at this time the prophet's widow

[1] The doctrine of Blood Atonement came into existence
in the Mormon church after the removal to Utah. Stated
briefly, it is that apostasy and all other sins against the
church are to be punished with death. The central idea of
it has thus been put by Brigham Young: "There are sins
that can be atoned for by an offering upon an altar, as in
ancient days; and there are sins that the blood of a lamb,
of a calf, or of turtle doves, cannot remit, but they must be
atoned for by the blood of man."

did not believe in the Mormon doctrine. Her son, Joseph, who in youth was constantly under her care and influence, did not consider himself a Mormon as late as 1853, when he reached his majority.   Meanwhile those of the Mormons hostile to Young (of whom there were ˉmany in Illinois, Iowa, and Wisconsin) were ineffectually striving to form a new religious society.   The chief difficulty was that too many aspired to the leadership.   Sidney Rigdon, failing of it, had retired with a few disciples to his old home in Pennsylvania.   James J. Strang—an elder under Joseph the prophet—conceiving a novel plan, had gone to Big Beaver Island, in Lake Michigan, where he had planted a Mormon colony, with himself at the head under the title of King Strang.   Here he flourished for a time, showing some ability as a ruler; but having countenanced polygamy, enjoined upon the women of his demesne the wearing of bloomers, and committed various other follies, he, like his celebrated predecessor and model, Smith, was assassinated, and his people dispersed.

At length an organization of the Saints was effected at Zarahelma, Wisconsin, and in April, 1860, Joseph Smith, Jr., consented to put himself at the head.   This he did only

after many solicitations. While he was pon-
dering the matter different plans of action
were proposed to him by admiring neighbors.
One was "to go to Utah, depose Brigham
Young, become rich, wed three or four wives,
and enjoy existence." On uniting with the
Mormons, Joseph Smith, Jr., agreed to remain
at Nauvoo for five years in order to try
whether the place could not again be made a
rallying point for the church. When the
news of this got abroad, a meeting was called
in hot haste by the gentiles of the country
round about, and resolutions passed protest-
ing against the return of the Mormons. At
a subsequent meeting it was even put to vote
and carried that "no Mormon should be permitted to preach or pray in the county."
Copies of these different resolutions were
formally served on Smith. He also received
letters threatening him with personal violence.

In 1865, the headquarters of the new church
were removed to Plano, Illinois. While here
Smith carefully questioned his mother on certain points respecting his father, the prophet,
about which there had been (and yet is) much
controversy. In this interview Emma Smith
said that the prophet had never had
any other wife; nor ever, so far as she
knew, had sustained unlawful relations to any

woman. She said also that she believed the church to have been established by divine direction. To use her own words: "Joseph Smith [unaided] could neither write nor dictate a coherent and well-worded letter, let alone dictating a book like the Book of Mormon. And although I was an active participant in the scenes that transpired, and was present during the translation of the plates, and had cognizance of things as they transpired, it is marvelous to me, 'a marvel and a wonder as much as to anybody else.'" Emma Smith said further concerning the composition of the Book of Mormon: "Joseph would dictate hour after hour; and when returning after meals, or after interruptions, he would at once begin where he had left off, without either seeing the manuscript or hearing any portion of it read to him. This was a usual thing for him to do. It would have been improbable that a learned man [of himself] could do this; and for one so ignorant and unlearned as he was, it was simply impossible." Plano continued to be the headquarters of the Reformed Mormon church until the year 1883, when they were again removed; this time to Lamoni, Iowa.

Facts such as the above, respecting a religious society almost unknown to the world, yet to-day vigorously at work about us, show the wonderful vitality of all forms of Mormonism. It is the object of the following sketch to afford what explanation of this vitality may lie in an exact portrayal of primitive Mormon life—of life in Nauvoo in the days of Joseph the prophet.

I.

NAUVOO means the Place Beautiful. There can be no doubt of this, for was not the interpretation by Joseph Smith, who founded and christened the town and who alone among men held the key to that cabalistic tongue, the Reformed Egyptian, whence the word was derived?[1]

But Nauvoo certainly is beautiful in its commanding situation on the Illinois bluffs. Before it, in a curve of great majesty,—convex toward the Iowa shore—sweeps the Mississippi. A level tract of country extends east from the river for a mile and a half, or to where a north and south line would form a chord connecting the extremities of the arc or curve which the river makes. An acclivity begins along this imaginary line and increases gradually until an elevation is reached of one hundred and forty feet from the river margin.

[1] An interesting surmise as to the origin of the word Nauvoo has been given the writer of this paper by Professor Toy, of Harvard. It is this: "There is a Hebrew word, nāweh, which means 'beautiful.' Nauvoo is not Hebrew in form, but might have been a mispronunciation of the word mentioned.'

On this elevation is the Nauvoo of to-day and
here in the past was the wide-famed Mormon
Temple.   But the Nauvoo of the past mainly
was on the flat between the river and the
acclivity.   Opposite Nauvoo are two features
which enter into the landscape with it : one,
a wide expanse of low land, upon which, near
the river, has been reared the hamlet of Montrose ; the other, a mass of bluff, which is to
the south of the hamlet, and springs boldly
up from the water's edge.   It is one hundred
and seventy-one feet to the top of this bluff,
and here many summer cottages have been
built ; here also yearly the Methodists hold
great camp meetings.   The view of Nauvoo
from the river is striking.   The town is distinctly visible, yet seems illusory and far
away.   The slope which it crowns is inclined
gently from the eye, and hence the streets
and buildings can be discerned with ease.
At the same time the distance is such as to
lend to the whole an air of remoteness and
insubstantiality.   Especially is this true on
days flooded with sunshine.   The place then
appears as though it were held aloft against
the blue sky in the grasp of some Colossus.
At the distance of the river, by far the most
noticeable object in Nauvoo is the spire of
the Catholic church of St. Mary.   This

church stands near the spot formerly
occupied by the Temple. Its spire is as
high as was that of the Temple (one hundred
and fifty feet) and serves, as did the Temple
spire, strongly to accentuate the landscape.
Up and down the Mississippi, and from
miles away in Iowa, it can be seen—a land-
mark lofty and impressive. In beholding it,
now in plain view, now lost, now in view again,
one can understand how the zealous Mormon
leaving Nauvoo an exile would turn to gaze
for the last time on the angel with golden
trumpet which surmounted the spire of the
Temple. Near St. Mary's, nestled among
evergreens and shrubs, is the convent of the
Benedictine sisters. In thus pitching upon
picturesque and commanding sites for their
ecclesiastical buildings the Catholic church
instructs all others. Throughout the great
valley of the Mississippi, at Dubuque, at
Muscatine, at many towns, the church
edifices, the convents, the schools of the great
Catholic organization may be seen occupying
the boldest bluffs, the most sightly elevations
—spots whence can be flung abroad over
woodland and meadow and stream the music
of their matin and vesper bells. In securing
a place for herself—at once so eligible and
so historic—in Nauvoo, the Catholic church

not only has followed a wise and time-honored custom, but has set a seal of triumph against not the least of her enemies.

To look down from the old Temple site on a day in early June is to witness a scene of great interest and animation. The flat is covered with strawberry fields, and scores of pickers are bending and crouched among the vines. So distant are they that they seem bees hovering among the sweets of the clover bloom. Beyond them is the swirling and eddying river; beyond the river is the bluff— Bluff Park it is called—where the camp-meetings are held, now embowered in green foliage, but disclosing glimpses of the white tents of the campers; and over all are the dazzling sunshine and the sweet, soft air. The evening hours at this season are not less enjoyable than those of the day. First comes the sunset, a royal pageant in scarlet in the far distant West. Could Joseph have been moved to his prophecy, that one day "the saints would become a mighty people in the midst of the Rocky Mountains," by fore-gleams of promise as to this western land in the Nauvoo sunsets? Later there is singing in Bluff Park, perhaps by a large congregation of worshipers, perhaps by a small company, and the tones come floating to the ear across

a space which so perfectly modulates and
harmonizes them that they seem to sustain
no relations to any purely human source.
The many camp fires which flash and
twinkle among the trees remind one of the
similar fires which a half century ago were
lighted on the same shore by the Mormon
exiles in the bleak, chill February nights
which they spent there in preparation for
their flight into the wilderness. Having retired to bed in a spacious chamber of one of
the old Mormon dwellings on the acclivity,
the traveler can often see from his window the
search-light of some approaching river packet
as, with the fierce eyeball of a Cyclops, it roves
along the channel and occasionally casts an
inquiring and all-revealing glance over the
land.

In the autumn there are other sights. The
great slope from the church of St. Mary to
the river, and the many lesser slopes into
which this great one is broken at the summit,
are covered with vineyards, and in the last
days of September and first days of October
come in endless profusion the purple and
white clusters of the Delaware, the Concord,
and the Catawba. The air is slumbrous and
full of haze; the river, Bluff Park, and the
fields lately rife with the bloom and fruit of

the strawberry, all are steeped in a mellow glory. To be in Nauvoo then is to be in Champagne or Burgundy. A large part of the grapes grown there are made into wine on the spot : into Catawba and other brands. Eighty thousand gallons are not an unusual product for a single season.

The Nauvoo of Mormon days was sparsely scattered over an area of some six or eight square miles. It was laid out in blocks of four acres, and each block was subdivided into four lots. In this way generous room for gardens was provided in connection with the dwellings. The principal street of the town was Main street, which extended north and south across the flat or peninsula, as it may be called, at a distance of a mile from the river. Another street of importance was Water street, which crossed Main at right angles, and was the street nearest the river on the southern side of the peninsula. There were eight streets running entirely across the peninsula north and south besides Main, and nineteen running east and west besides Water. The names of some of the former were Partridge, Carlin, Granger, and Bain ; of some of the latter—familiar because of having belonged to distinguished Mormons—Taylor, Carlos, Hyrum, Joseph, Young, Knight, Ripley,

Munson, Kimball, and Parley. The Temple stood in the centre of a block facing on Wells street, a thoroughfare that because of the broken nature of the ground was only partially completed. Back of it were the similar uncompleted streets, Woodruff, Page, Barnett, and others. The population of Nauvoo in its prime (1844) was perhaps not far from ten or twelve thousand persons. Its numbers frequently have been put at fifteen or twenty thousand, but with exaggeration. Its growth had been rapid in the extreme. In the summer of 1839 there were but a few log buildings. By June, 1840, two hundred and fifty buildings of log, frame, and brick had been erected and more were under way. During the years from 1840 to 1844 nearly four thousand persons were added to the population of Nauvoo from foreign lands. A short distance south of the town was discovered and opened a quarry of hard limestone suitable for the best uses of architecture. Steam saw mills were set up. There were also put in operation a steam flour mill, a tool factory, a foundry, and a manufactory of china ware. A steam boat owned and navigated by Mormons plied between Nauvoo and Fulton, Fort Madison, Keokuk, Warsaw, and other adjacent villages on the Mississippi.

Capping all, two regular publications—the *Times and Seasons* and the *Nauvoo Neighbor*—were issued, and found readers as far east as Philadelphia and Boston.   At the time of the Exodus of the Mormons in 1846, an eye witness of events counted from the roof of the Temple two thousand houses in the city proper and in the suburbs five hundred more. One half of these were mere shanties built some of logs and some of poles plastered over; others were framed.   Of the remainder about twelve hundred were tolerably fit dwellings; six hundred of them at least were good brick or frame structures.   The number of buildings made wholly of brick was about five hundred, a goodly proportion of them large and handsome.

To-day Nauvoo is a town of twelve hundred people.   To the visitor the evidences of former and long departed prosperity present themselves on every hand.   At the foot of Main street, to the left as one faces the river, stands the unfinished Nauvoo house, the hotel commanded by Jehovah in a vision to Joseph Smith to be built "for the boarding of strangers," and in which, according to the prophet's interpretation of Jehovah's words, he (the prophet) "and his seed after him were to have place from generation to gene-

ration, forever and ever." The building as
projected, and in part laid out, was large. Not
all of the foundation even was laid at the
time of the Exodus; but the south-west angle
was partly completed and exhibits in the
brick and stone work traces of superior me-
chanical skill. The bricks especially are
seen to have been laid with a precision and
pointed with a skill hard to be excelled.
The rooms within the completed part are lofty
and spacious, and look forth upon the hurry-
ing river not forty feet away. Emma Smith,
the wife of the prophet, the *electra* Cyria or
elect lady of his writings, lived for some
years in these rooms after the murder of her
husband. One block to the north of the
crumbling Nauvoo House is the frame building known as the Mansion House, in which
the prophet lived and kept tavern while awaiting the completion of his permanent abode.
The rooms of this house also are large; in one
of them is a closet which on casual inspection
seems to be a very ordinary affair, but which
has its secret. Protruding from cross pieces
fastened against its four sides are wooden pegs
for the support of clothing. Pull out (as
you can if you wish to try) from the cross
piece on the left hand side of the closet the
further peg, then strike upward the cross

piece itself.   It will respond to your blow by
rising on a pivot, and the top edge of a low
door will be revealed.   This door when
opened discloses a shaft just large enough to
contain a perpendicular ladder reaching to
the loft of the house.   When Joseph Smith
was being hotly pursued by the authorities of
Illinois in 1842–3 on requisition from the governor of Missouri, his whereabouts were often
difficult to fix.   That he was somewhere on his
own premises was suspected.   That he was in
the loft of his dwelling would seem strongly
to be indicated by the existence of the
contrivance for concealment just described.
Across Main street from the Nauvoo House
is the old, weather-beaten frame building
in which Emma Smith, the wife of the
prophet, passed many of the declining years
of her life.   This building with the land about
it was the first piece of property bought by
the prophet on reaching Nauvoo.   In the
door-yard, directly above the river and
shielded by shrubbery, are the graves of
Emma Smith and of other members of the
prophet's family.

Looking up Main street the visitor sees a
goodly number of large and substantial but
widely separated brick edifices.   Among them
are the Hall which was used by the Mormon

Masonic order and the residences which were occupied by Brigham Young and the Elders, Kimball and Pratt.   Young's residence, like the most of those built by the Mormons, is protected by quaintly notched fire walls above the gables—such walls as are to be seen above the old Boston State House and in prints of the old parts of cities in Europe.   The house of John D. Lee—the Mormon Bishop so notorious in connection with the Mountain Meadow massacre—which for a long time stood on Carlin street, has been torn down. The Hall of the Seventies, which marked the corner of Granger and Kimball streets, also has been removed.   Of the Council House, in which religious and other meetings were held during the erection of the Temple, and which stood at the intersection of Water and Granger streets, only the foundation remains. The office of the *Times and Seasons* was one block west of the Council House on Water and Bain streets.   It has been removed from this site, and is now in another part of the town. The office of the *Nauvoo Expositor*—famous for the issue of a solitary edition ere its type were pied in the street by order of the indignant prophet, whom it had assailed for immoral practices—still stands in its original place on Mulholland street near Temple

square. Just west of Temple square, and
down the acclivity from it in the same enclosure with the convent of the Benedictine
Sisters, is the small stone structure—now used
for a stable—in which the military organization of Nauvoo—the celebrated Nauvoo Legion—kept their arms and other accoutre-
ments. The wide gaps and spaces now ex-
isting between the different buildings that
have come down from Mormon days—on
Main street especially—have been caused by
the decay and removal of the structures of
logs and boards which once closed them up.
Of the buildings removed some are to be
found across the river in Montrose, whither
they have been transported in winter time
upon the ice. All about Nauvoo, on the acclivity and on the flat, are to be found the
partially obliterated traces of old walls and
cellars betokening the great decrease in the
number of places for habitation which the
years have brought since the departure of the
Mormons. It is little short of startling that
Salt Lake City—the site of which, when
chosen by the exiles from Nauvoo, was yet
hardly within the United States and was a
thousand miles from the nearest civilization,
should for many years have been connected
with the rest of the world by railroads; while

Nauvoo itself continues to be brought into outside relations only by the Mississippi river. With this thought in mind, it does not seem so strange that there should be persons in Nauvoo to-day who almost wish the exiles back again.

The Mormon Temple, as has been said, stood in the centre of Temple square on Wells street. Not a vestige of its walls or of the stone blocks, which composed its walls, is now to be found there. The spot is covered in part by houses and in part by outbuildings and the *debris* of back yards. A structure as light and perishable as the frame dwelling first owned by the prophet in Nauvoo still stands, but the great Temple with its steps, its pilasters, and its tower, has disappeared forever. During the Mormon exodus it was sold to a French communistic society, called Icarians, under the leadership of Etienne Cabet; and, while under their control, in November, 1848, was destroyed by fire with the exception of the bare walls. In 1850, three of these went down before a tornado, which the Icarians described as of frightful sublimity. The fourth or west wall remained in place some years longer, being strongly joined at the sides to an interior wall parallel with it. The only picture of the ruins of the Temple, which exists exhibits this west wall surrounded at the base by heaped and broken masonry. For many years these ruins—like those of the Roman Coliseum—were a stone quarry for other edifices. There is hardly a building of any pretensions in Nauvoo, erected within the last forty years, which has not somewhere, in its foundation or super-structure, stone from the Mormon Temple. It is a hard white stone susceptible of hand-some finish. The post-office is built of it almost entirely, and it is to be found in the walls of churches and of the huge wine cel-lars. In 1860, the remaining fragments were carted from the Temple site and pitched helter-skelter into an orchard lot owned by one of Nauvoo's oldest residents. There they can be seen now: clock face, (for the Temple had a clock among its embellishments) quaint, sun-visaged, pilaster, capitals, and much besides.

Visiting this orchard one bright spring day, I seated myself on a stone block, in somewhat the mood of Macaulay's famous New Zea-lander, and drifted into retrospect. It was the 6th of April, 1841,—the day on which the corner-stones of the Temple were to be laid in place. Approaching Nauvoo from Carth-age and from other points eastward were farm vehicles in great numbers and of every kind, bringing crowds to celebrate the event. Boats brought many from Warsaw, from Fort Madison, and from Montrose. The town was *en fête*. The Nauvoo Legion paraded in full strength, with new arms and new uniforms. Lieutenant-General Joseph Smith, resplendent in gold cord and cocked hat and escorted by an equally resplendent staff, rode through the streets. Everywhere cheers greeted him. There were martial music and thunder of cannon. The ladies of Nauvoo presented a flag to the Legion. A procession was formed, and the line of march taken to the site of the Temple. The site reached, hymns were sung, and President Sidney Rigdon made an address. The architect lowered the first stone—the one at the southeast corner of the edifice—into position. The prophet, who had laid aside his military regalia, blessed the stone in these words: "This principal corner-stone in representation of the first presidency is now duly laid in honor of the great God; and may it there remain until the whole fabric is completed; and may the same be accomplished speedily that the Saints may have a place to worship God and the Son of Man have where to lay his head."

From the 6th of April, 1841, it now came to be the 24th of May, 1845. It was six o'clock on a clear and beautiful morning.

The walls of the Temple were up, and the cap-stone ready to be put in place. The ceremonies were directed by the Twelve headed by President Brigham Young, and a great crowd of the Saints were gathered on the slope of the acclivity to witness them. On the summit of the west wall a band of musicians played national and religious airs. The stone was brought forward, and the crowd broke forth "into shouts of Grace, Grace unto it!" It was lowered into position, and this shout was exchanged for "Hosanna to God and the Lamb! Amen! and Amen!" repeated three times—an acclaim, which seemed not only to give joy on earth, but to fill the heavens with gladness. A hymn rose on the air:

" Have you heard the revelation
Of this latter dispensation
Which is unto every Nation,
  Oh! prepare to meet thy God?

We are a band of brethren,
And we rear the Lord a temple,
And the cap-stone now is finished,   .
And we'll sound the news abroad."

The Temple, the structure which, it was proudly claimed, exhibited more of revelation, more of splendor, and more of God than all others in the world, was standing before me in completed outline. Supporting the cornice were the thirty hewn stone pilasters; the base of each a crescent moon; the capital of each a sun, with human face surmounted by two hands holding trumpets. There were the two great stories and two half stories; the four tiers of windows, gothic and round in alternation; the golden letters, "Holiness to the Lord," above the entrance; and, soaring one hundred feet over all into the blue sky, the spire.

Bringing now my revery to an end, for the sun had gone down, I rose with the thought: So long past are Mormon days in the Northwest that their occurrences, like those of other days of the same period the world over, begin to take on an air of strangeness and of romance.[1]

[1] Upon an old building in Nauvoo, situated at the corner of Mulholland and Woodruff streets, which at one time was the abode of the officers of the Icarian society, may be read the following inscription: " *Celui qui a pris l'honneur d'une personne ne peut plus rien lui prendre.*" [In good English paraphrase: "He who filches from me my good name takes that which . . . . makes me poor indeed."] Elsewhere in Nauvoo a German who, through much litigation over a title, became deeply impressed with the fleeting character of earthly possessions, has thus recorded himself on the weather-boards of his house just beneath the western gable:

"*Das haus ist mein, und doch nicht mein;
    Wer nach mir kommt wird auch so sein.*"

[This house is mine and yet not mine. It will be the same with him who shall own it after me.] From all of which it appears that the Mormons have not been the only people with peculiarities who have dwelt in the Place Beautiful.

II.

The founder of Mormonism and its first Prophet was Joseph Smith. He it was who built Nauvoo, and he it was in obedience to whom missionaries went forth to Europe, to Palestine and to the islands of the sea. To say of him that he was one of the most successful impostors of modern times—probably as little self-deceived as any man that ever has lived—is not to do him injustice. To say of him also that he possessed something akin to genius in his comprehension of, and power over, a certain simple-minded, usually honest class of people, but superstitious and fanatical, is merely to accord him his due. It hardly is a fair explanation of his supremacy during the Nauvoo period to state, as does John Hay in the *Atlantic Monthly*, that "a little brains went further in Nauvoo than anywhere else on earth," yet the jest is not without its critical value.

As a youth, Smith has been described by ex-Gov. Harding, of Utah Territory, who often saw him in his native town of Palmyra, New York. He was six feet tall, long-limbed, and with big feet; his hair a light auburn; his eyes large and of a bluish gray color; his nose prominent; his face pale and unbearded, and his mouth a study. The same man says further concerning him that he was a lazy boy; spent his time largely in fishing; rarely smiled; never quarreled or fought; was hard on bird's nests; and so constitutionally and inveterately untruthful that in the town where he lived it was a common observation on any improbable tale that it was as big a lie as young Joe ever told. Nor, seemingly, were his parents and his brothers held in any better esteem in Palmyra than was he. Mr. Pomeroy Tucker, who personally knew them all, says of them in his book on Mormonism: "The Smith family were popularly regarded as an illiterate, whiskey drinking, shiftless, irreligious race of people; and," he adds, "Joseph was unanimously voted the laziest and most worthless of the generation." This statement may be supplemented by the final one, that a written declaration of the untruthfulness and viciousness of the entire Smith family was, in 1833, made and signed by sixty-two of the best citizens of Palmyra and repeatedly has been published. But, despite all his personal and family drawbacks, Smith forged rapidly to the front. He pretended to be able to locate hidden treasures by the aid of a witch-hazel rod, and finding certain of his neighbors credulous enough to believe

him, was emboldened to try something greater.
One day he came into his father's house at
the dinner hour holding a package concealed
under his coat. To the somewhat natural
enquiry of the family as to what it was, he
replied that it was a golden Bible. This reply
meeting with some favor, he refused to show
what he really had, but followed up the advantage gained by circulating reports as to his
Bible discovery among the towns-people. The
sort of people some of those were who, in the
little town of Palmyra, and in the country
about it, listened to Smith may be inferred
from their behavior when under religious excitement. They would run through the fields,
get upon stumps, preach to imaginary con-
gregations, enter the water; would make the
most ridiculous grimaces, creep upon their
hands and feet, and roll on the frozen ground.
At the dead hour of night, young men among
them might be seen running over the fields
and hills in pursuit of, as they said, balls of
fire which they had detected moving in the
atmosphere.

Smith's influence over a mind at all
superstitious—even when sound in other
ways—is shown by the infatuation into which
he drew his townsman Martin Harris; an
infatuation which led Harris to exhaust his

hard earned means in publishing the Book of Mormon.   To Harris's believing ears—as often as was necessary in order to keep him to the work—we may imagine the cunning Joseph to have repeated the marvelous tale of how, amid thick darkness, a pillar of light had descended until it fell about him revealing two personages whose brightness and glory defied all description, one of whom pointing to the other had said : "This is my beloved son, hear him!"   But illustrations of Smith's ingenuity and cleverness in advancing his own fortunes abound.   Thus in 1830 he announced himself as in receipt of a revelation consecrating and setting apart his wife Emma as an elect lady.   She was to be supported from the church and to "let her soul delight in her husband."   Thus also in 1836, in Kirtland, Ohio, when the money resources of the Saints were at an exceptionally low ebb, the prophet received a timely revelation commanding the establishment of the Kirtland Safety Society anti-Banking Company— an institution which, after unlawfully putting in circulation a large quantity of bills, was brought to a stop by proceedings in the courts. On the march from Kirtland to Missouri in 1834, there were a number of occurrences demonstrating, not only the infatuation of

the Saints, but as well, their poverty of humor.
Coming one day to a large prehistoric mound,
the prophet ordered it to be opened.   A little
beneath the surface the bones of a human
skeleton were found.   These the prophet
declared to be the remains of a Lamanite
warrior and chieftain whose name was Selaph,
and who had been killed in the last struggle
between the Lamanites and Nephites.   On
another occasion a large black snake was discovered near the road.   Martin Harris, whose
confidence in the possession by Joseph and
his disciples of the power to work miracles
was yet unshaken, removed his shoes and
stockings and, commanding the reptile not to
do him harm, somewhat gingerly presented
his toes to its head.   The snake remained
quiet, and Harris loudly proclaimed a victory
over serpents.   But, on repeating this test of
miraculous power in the case of another snake,
he received a wound in the ankle.   This was
satisfactorily accounted for by the prophet,
who imputed to Harris a weakened faith.   It
was while on this first journey westward from
Kirtland that Smith defined an angel as "a
tall, slim, well built, handsome man·with a
bright pillar upon his head."

On the advent of Joseph Smith at the place
which he forthwith named Nauvoo, and whither

both he and his followers had fled from real
persecution in Missouri, revelations to meet
present exigencies and requirements came
rapidly. First among them was the injunction to build a house unto the name of Joseph
—the Nauvoo House; next an injunction to
build a house unto the name of Joseph for the
most High to dwell therein—the Temple. To
defray the cost of the latter "the Saints from
afar" are bidden to come with all their gold,
silver, precious stones, and antiquities; to
bring the box tree, the fir tree, and the pine
tree; together with iron, copper, brass, and
zinc. As a means of preventing delay in the
work, the Saints are told that only a speci-
fied time is allowed them by Jehovah in which
to finish the Temple; after the expiration
of that time, their baptisms for the dead
and their prayers will be absolutely unaccept-
able. The medium chosen for getting these
important revelations before the people of
Nauvoo was the semi-monthly periodical and
newspaper—the *Times and Seasons*. The editor of this paper more than once found it
necessary strongly to emphasize the penalties
prescribed by Jehovah for neglect of his com-
mands. Thus, in December, 1841, word was
published that because of the sloth and disobe-
dience of certain Saints, grave doubts were

felt by the authorities of the church as to the propriety of any longer administering to any Saint the rite of baptism. For, it was convincingly argued, if the whole church with her dead " is to be rejected of God for the sins of a few, she may as well be rejected without baptism as with it." In the same issue containing the above appeared a list of such offerings and services as were in immediate demand. Among the offerings named were beds, bedding, socks, mittens, shoes, clothing, and provisions of all kinds; among the services named were those of stone cutters, quarrymen, and teams and teamsters. In June, 1842, another appeal had to be made. This time it was put in poetic form.

" Prepare for that glory the prophets once saw,"
    (Sang the editor of the *Times and Seasons*.)
"And bring on your gold and your precious
        things too,
    As tithes for the Temple of God at Nauvoo."

Even this did not wholly suffice, for in August, 1844, an editorial appeared under the sinister heading, "A Word to the Wise." From it the fact was learned that Joseph had had a revelation respecting tithing ; and so explicit was the language of this revelation " that he who ran might read it and a fool need not err." The language in question was to the effect that the Lord required of his Saints, for the building of his House, all their surplus property, and, after that, "one tenth of all their interest annually."

But the *Times and Seasons* is of more interest to us now as a mirror of Mormon life and practices in Nauvoo than as a medium of revelations. In its columns we find many things not wanting in unconscious humor. For example, one of the early editors (Don Carlos Smith) gravely assures his readers that no pains will be spared by him to make the paper both interesting and valuable; for through it he aims at nothing less than the salvation of the human family. A month later he gives somewhat in detail the plan upon which he will work. He will advocate the doctrines of the church of Jesus Christ of Latter Day Saints, soliciting original essays of a nature " Eclectic, Analectic, and Analytic." In his efforts for the regeneration of the world, Don Carlos met with the discouragements inseparable from large enterprises. At least this seems fairly to be inferred from such a remark in his columns as: "Printers like all other men live by eating; and in cold weather fire is very useful;" or from such a remark as: "It has been so long

since we have had any honey that we are very
certain we should not refuse any if it were
offered us, especially if it were clear and
nice;" or from such another remark as:
"Those of our subscribers who are delinquent
and who live in this vicinity can bring us, in
payment, wood or any kind of produce, as
these things are very necessary in a family."
As Nauvoo increased in size, it naturally offered
a field for various useful and ornamental trades;
and it was also natural that these trades should
be represented in the *Times and Seasons* by
advertisements. Among these advertisements
was the card of a tailor announcing the latest
fashions direct from Philadelphia; the card of
a dress-maker begging to inform the ladies of
Nauvoo that she stood prepared to render them
valuable service in her art, and further that
she had had several years experience therein
under a French modiste; the card of a sur-
geon dentist "from Berlin in Prussia, late of
Liverpool and Preston, England," who awaited
patronage at the house of Brigham Young and
whose "charges were strictly moderate;" the
card of a solitary attorney-at-law, with office
near the Temple; lastly the card of a druggist
and physician who had for sale Vancouver's
powders for the immediate cure of the fever
and ague and who ought to have had patron-

age, if anybody ought, for in that part of Nauvoo built on the flat, fever and ague prevailed much of the time. But doctors were not popular with the Saints, we are editorially informed in the *Times and Seasons*, for the reason that the latter prefer as a dependence in sickness "the commandments of God to an arm of flesh." Poetry, as has been seen, was not an art despised in Nauvoo. Its leading devotee was Eliza R. Snow. She gave the muse little rest. She had something in nearly every number of the *Times and Seasons*. She celebrated in execrable verse everything from President William Henry Harrison to the Nauvoo Legion. But, bad as she was, there was one rhymster in Nauvoo who was worse. This was Elder Partridge, who one day in April, 1840, delivered himself of the following concerning the hardships endured by the Saints in Missouri :

"They have been tarr'd, feather'd, and often
    times whip'd.
    Been murder'd and plunder'd and robb'd,
    and driv'n.
  Their houses destroy'd till they have been strip'd
    Of all earthly wealth, but they've treasures in
    heav'n."

It was not alone by poetizing that the Saints manifested an interest in culture.

They founded a university. Its curriculum was extensive, including arithmetic, algebra, plane and analytical geometry, conic sections, plane, spherical, and analytical trigonometry, mensuration, surveying, navigation, the differential and integral calculus, astronomy, chemistry, and mental philosophy. But more surprising than all else is the fact that these numerous branches of learning were classed as English literature, and taught by one man —Professor Orson Pratt. The tuition of students was announced in the *Times ana Seasons* to be five dollars per quarter, payable semi-quarterly in advance. Liberal as was the encouragement given by the church to science and letters, it believed in rigorousness in respect to conduct. It dictated to, anathematized, and excommunicated refractory members with an assumption of omnipotence worthy the best days of the Papacy. Thus, on September 28, 1841, Elder James M. Henderson is ordered by the Quorum of Seventies to come home immediately. On November 15, 1841, it is unanimously voted at a council of the First Presidency and of the Twelve that John E. Page return to Nauvoo without delay. In January, 1842, Elder A. Lits is ordered to come to Nauvoo immediately to answer charges which may be pre-

ferred against him; and Dr. Benjamin Winchester is silenced from preaching until he
makes satisfaction for disobeying the instruc-
tions delivered to him by the Presidency.   In
July, 1842, notice is given that Dr. Benjamin
Winchester, having repented and recanted, is
restored to his former fellowship in the church.
On November 23, 1844, it is resolved by the
High Council that Amos B. Tomlinson and
Ebenezer Robinson and wife be cast off from
the church of Jesus Christ of Latter Day
Saints for apostasy, and that notice of the fact
be published in the *Times and Seasons*. Along
with, yet in strange contrast, to items such as
the foregoing, we read on January 1, 1841,
that " a late arrival at New Orleans states that
in October past there was a French frigate at
St. Helena to take the remains of Napoleon
to France."

But meantime Nauvoo had waxed great,
and with it Joseph the prophet. A charter
for the town had been obtained from the
admiring people of Illinois, under which the
municipality was almost independent of the
state.   The formation of the Nauvoo Legion
had been authorized, and the prophet had
been commissioned its Lieutenant-General,
and John C. Bennet, at that time the prophet's
main dependence, its Major-General. Letters

mailed at Nauvoo bore the proud address,
The City of Joseph. The New York *Herald*
called Smith the Western Mahomet, the
Prophet of America. Besides the land bought
in Illinois for the site of Nauvoo, several thousand acres had been bought or contracted for
by the Saints near the village of Keokuk in
Iowa. In a word, preparations for the founding of something like a Mormon Empire on
the banks of the Mississippi were well advanced. The vital importance, in state and
congressional elections, of the three thousand
Mormon votes of Nauvoo and vicinity, which
were always cast as the prophet directed, had
come to be recognized by candidates; and
political parties vied with each other in bid-
ding for the prophet's favor. On the one
hand, he was assiduously courted by Douglas
and the democrats; while, on the other, Lincoln sent him pamphlets and strove to attach
him to the whigs. Douglas, however, was in
a position to render him the most aid, and
hence was most to his mind. He pronounced
him a master spirit. In 1839 Smith had gone
to Washington to see President Van Buren
concerning the outrages perpetrated on the
Mormons by the Missourians, but had got no
satisfaction. Accordingly, when the presidential election of 1844 was approaching, he

made it his business to sound the different candidates for their views on the Mormon question.   He wrote to John C. Calhoun, Lewis Cass, Richard M. Johnson, Henry Clay, and Martin Van Buren.   Calhoun and Clay courteously responded, but intimated the impropriety in their formulating definitive views on the question at that time.   Smith's replies to these gentlemen are curiosities in epistolary composition.   In the one to Calhoun this characteristic passage is found: "While I have power of body and mind—while water runs and grass grows—while virtue is lovely and vice hateful—and while a stone points out a spot where a fragment of American liberty once was, I or my posterity will plead the cause of injured innocence, until Missouri makes atonement for all her sins, or sinks disgraced, degraded, and damned to hell, where the worm dieth not and the fire is not quenched."   The letter in reply to Clay is addressed to "that great plenipotentiary, the renowned secretary of state, the ignoble duelist, the gambling senator, and the whig candidate for the presidency, Henry Clay."

Disgusted with his appeals for light from the various presidential candidates, the prophet resolved to test the feelings of the American people by running for the presidency himself.

"Who shall be our next president?" defiantly asked the *Times and Seasons* of February 1, 1844. "We have our eye on the man; we shall notify our friends in due time, and when we do we shall take a long pull, a strong pull, and a pull altogether." On March 1, 1844, this intimation was followed by the announcement, in big type: "For President, General Joseph Smith, Nauvoo, Illinois." Later (on May 17th) some sort of a national convention was got together in Nauvoo, and Joseph put in formal nomination before the country.

As the prophet increased in years and good fortune a corresponding elation was perceptible in his manner. In public discourse he was easy and complacent, seeming to feel the importance of his position; in private talk he was, in general, agreeable, but, if opposed, was apt to be loud and truculent. A man who on one occasion chanced to be on the Mississippi steamboat which the Mormons owned and navigated encountered Smith among the passengers, and heard his converse. He afterwards said of him: "In his repeated treatment of those who did not acknowledge his pretensions, he exemplified an assertion of his own, namely, that in order to get through the world to the best advantage, he had learned to browbeat his way."

Many stories are told concerning his skill and invincibility as an athlete. Says the ex-Utah Congressional delegate, George Q. Cannon: "On Saturday, the 28th day of January, 1843, the prophet played a fine game of ball at Nauvoo with his brethren. On Monday, the 13th day of March, 1843, he met William Wall, a most expert wrestler of Ramus, Illinois, and had a friendly bout with him. He easily conquered Wall, who up to that time had been a champion. About the same time he had a contest at pulling sticks with Justus A. Morse, reputed to be the strongest man in the region. The prophet used but one hand and easily defeated Morse." His aplomb, under almost any circumstances, was astonishing. Thus, on being asked by an English traveler which of the Trinity had appeared to him on the occasion of the first revelation, he at once replied: "It was the Father, with the Son on his right hand, and he said: 'I am the Father, and this Being on my right hand is my Son, Jesus Christ.'" Again, in preaching on one occasion, he made the statement that baptism was essential to salvation. "Stop!" cried a Methodist clergyman who was among the listeners, "What do you say to the case of the penitent thief? You know our Savior said to the thief: 'This day shalt thou be

with me in Paradise,' which shows that he
could not have been baptized before his
admission." "How do you know," quickly
retorted Smith, "that he wasn't baptized
before he became a thief? But," continued
he, frowning down the merriment which his
sally had excited, "this is not the true answer.
In the original Greek the word that has been
translated paradise means simply a place of
departed spirits. To that place the penitent
thief was conveyed, and there doubtlessly he
received the baptism necessary for his
admission to the heavenly kingdom." That
in his relations to the women of Nauvoo there
was much freedom seems to be established by
a great variety of proof. Stenhouse, the apos-
tate Mormon author, writing in 1870, says:
"There are now probably about a dozen sisters in Utah who proudly acknowledge themselves to be the wives of Joseph; and how
many others there may have been who held
that relationship no man knoweth." In person, at this period, Smith had grown fat; he
displayed a taste for jewelry; and his glance
is said to have been furtive and hard to fix.
But Josiah Quincy, of Massachusetts, who
met him shortly before his assassination, says
that he was a fine looking man, and that "one
could not resist the impression that capacity

and resource were natural to his stalwart person." Summing up his career to the time when he became a presidential candidate, Stenhouse says: "The poor farm laborer merges in the preacher; the preacher becomes a translator, a prophet, a seer, a revelator, a banker, an editor, a mayor, a lieutenant-general, a candidate for the presidency of the world's greatest republic; and, last of all, though not the least difficult of his achievements, he becomes the husband of many wives."

Polygamy was not an avowed institution among the Mormons until the Utah period. Its origin among them as a practice, and also, secretly, as a doctrine, was in the years spent in Nauvoo. The steps in its development were substantially as follows : Certain elders who were regretting that their union with their wives, in whom they had chanced to be exceptionally fortunate, would terminate with the present life, conceived the novel idea of being remarried for eternity. A ceremony to this end accordingly was performed. Thereupon certain other elders, whose conjugal relations were not so satisfactory, suggested that they be permitted to lighten their burden by contracting with some of their sisters in the faith, more · congenial to them than their wives, an alliance

actually to be enjoyed only in the world
to come, but prospectively to be enjoyed
here.   No objection being made to this
proposal, it was carried out.   In the words of
Joseph Smith, Jr., "spiritual affinities were
sought after ; the hitherto sacred precincts of
home were invaded ; less and less restraint
was exercised ; the lines between virtue and
license, before sharply drawn, grew more and
more indistinct.   Spiritual companionship for
the world to come, deriving its sanction from
an earthly priesthood, might (it was thought)
under the same sanction, be antedated and
put to actual test here; . . . . a wife in fact
was supplemented by one in spirit who in
easy transition became one in fact also.

Some examples of the working of this
doctrine of plurality among the Saints are
given by Mrs. Emily M. Austin.   Mrs. Austin
was a respectable woman who joined the
Mormons before their removal to Missouri.
She afterwards lived much in Nauvoo, taught
school there, and became well known.   She
did not go to Utah, and only recently
has died.   She has left a small book
(comparatively scarce) entitled " Life Among
the Mormons," in which she speaks from a
knowledge personal and direct.   "A note
was sent to me [one day]," she says in

this book, "desiring my attendance at a wedding at Deacon Lovey's. I at once began to question who it could be. There was no one in Deacon Lovey's family who was old enough to marry, thought I. However, I attended at the hour appointed, and when the parties advanced, it [sic] was Deacon Lovey himself, leading an old maid by the name of Elmyra Mack. I was more astonished now than I ever was. There sat his other wife looking perfectly happy. The ceremony was said, after which a lively time ensued, and all seemed joyous and full of merriment." Elsewhere in her book she says: "[On one occasion], while I stopped a few moments in conversation with Mrs. S——, her husband rode up in a splendid carriage and asked if I would not ride, as he was going on business the way I was to return. I accepted the offer, and on our way he asked if I had tried to inform myself of the great work which was enjoined upon us as God's children? I told him I knew of nothing but to serve God with an honest and upright heart. 'This is not all,' he said; 'God's work is progressive, ever onward. As his children grow more numerous their wants increase. He does for us all we wish or desire, if we trust in Him. He has promised us all things, if we live faithful to

Him. And now, since these promises are left us for our benefit, why not accept?' 'Accept what?' I asked. 'Accept and obey God's command,' he replied, 'which He has given through His servant Joseph ; that is, a man can have all the wives he can get, if he marries them for time and eternity ; that is, if he takes care of them in time, they will also be his in eternity ; for the glory of man is the woman ; the more women he has the more glory will crown him in heaven. And now, if when you consider this properly, you think it better to have one who will provide for and protect you, let me know your mind, and all will be well.'"

But although the prophet (to recur to Stenhouse's graphic phrase), in addition to being a candidate for the presidency, had achieved the glory of becoming the husband of many wives, foes were at work against him ; foes among the Saints and foes among the gentiles. Trouble, the result of rivalry, long since had broken out between him and his lieutenant John C. Bennett, and Bennett had gone to the East. Certain influential persons (among them William Law, Wilson Law, and Dr. R. D. Foster) had been cut off from the church, and were bitterly hostile. Among the gentiles a long-brewing fear and dislike of the Mormons, engendered by political and other causes, was manifesting itself. Into the midst of all this came, as a spark to a magazine of powder, the *Expositor* incident of June 7th, 1845. The Laws and others had established a newspaper called the *Nauvoo Expositor*. It professed belief in the Mormon doctrines, but repudiated the claims of Smith. As a vulnerable point in Smith's character, it assailed his chastity. Thereupon the excitement in Nauvoo was tremendous. The city council, under the lead of the prophet, met and, after much inflammatory talk, voted the *Expositor* and its office a public nuisance and ordered them abated. This order not being complied with by the proprietors, the press and type of the paper were pitched into the street by the prophet's deputies and destroyed. Following upon this, came the arrest of Smith and his brother Hyrum by a constable of the county, and their prompt release under a writ of *habeas corpus* issued by the Nauvoo municipal council. Such a direct defiance of the authority of the state by the Mormons, as was the delivery under this writ, roused great resentment among the gentiles. "Citizens!" exclaimed the *Warsaw Signal*, anent the occurrence, "arise, one and all! . . . We have no time for comment : every man will make his own.   Let it be made with powder and ball !" Governor Ford was appealed to.   He came to Carthage, the county seat, made a show of military force, and the two Smiths, after some negotiations, surrendered themselves into the Governor's hands and were lodged in the Carthage jail.   Meanwhile armed bands were congregating at several points in anticipation of orders to attack Nauvoo.   The Mormon leaders having given themselves up, these bands were now directed by the governor to disperse.   Many of them did so ; others were not thus to be cheated of their prey.   On June 27th, in the governor's absence at Nauvoo whither he had gone to make an address to the citizens, a mob collected from the direction of Warsaw.   Rolling into Carthage, it made straight for the jail, put aside the feeble guard it found there, and rushed towards the room on the upper floor in which were confined Joseph and Hyrum Smith. They heard the mob coming and threw their bodies against the door to bar ingress.   Several shots were fired by the mob through the door panels ; the door itself was then burst open and more shots fired.   One of them killed Hyrum Smith.   The prophet was not so easily disposed of.   He stood by the door

jamb and returned the fire. He fired four
shots and at each a man went down. Then,
wounded and bewildered, he rushed to a
window in the room which had been opened
to admit the soft June air, and half leaped,
half fell, into the yard below. Here, while
gathering himself into a sitting posture
against the well curb, a squad of his old
enemies, the Missourians, which was standing
by, discharged their pieces at him and he
dropped back dead.   .

III.

The death of Joseph Smith was the beginning of the end of Mormonism in Nauvoo.
He was succeeded, it is true, by Brigham
Young, but the glory of Zion was grown dim.
The times were troubled. In the church
there were dissensions; in both the church and
the town there was lawlessness. Horse stealing, grave robbing, and other forms of theft
were frequently practiced. So fearful were
the family of Joseph that the remains of the
prophet and his brother would be stolen,
if the place of their burial were known, that
a deception was practiced at the funeral. The
caskets, when borne from the Mansion House,
did not contain the dead. In the room of
the bodies bags of sand had been put; and

the caskets thus filled were deposited in a double vault, which had been excavated in the hill side some two hundred feet south of the Temple. This vault was encased by stone walls and closed by iron doors. The bodies themselves were secretly buried at night by Emma Smith, the prophet's wife. Where they were buried no one but she and her sons knew then ; and no one but the two sons who survive her, Joseph and Alexander, know now.

Besides theft, offenses against society in and about Nauvoo of a much darker sort marked the year immediately following the prophet's death. There were bold robberies and still bolder assassinations. From the time of the trouble in Missouri a secret organization was thought to have existed among the Saints, called the Sons of Dan or Danites. Certain early Mormon apostates had made oath, before a Congressional investigating committee, to the existence of such a society. Its object, they had said, was to drive out dissenters from the church. If any, on being notified to go, refused, they were secretly put to death. Nehemiah Odell, who had been examined before the Congressional committee, had said that he was present on one occasion during the war with the Missourians, when a company of the Danites received

the following somewhat remarkable command
from their Captain: "In the name of Laza-
rus, God, and the Lamb, fire! Danites."

To the Mormons—especially as represented
in the Danite Band—it has been the habit to
ascribe the perpetration of the thefts, robberies, and murders which were now plaguing
the vicinity of Nauvoo. That any such organization as this was at all active, or even existed, among the Mormons during the Nauvoo
period, there is virtually no proof. That such
an organization had existed, and that it was
revived in Utah, is a different proposition.
The most reasonable explanation of the Nauvoo outrages would seem to be that they
came of general border lawlessness. The
suspicion which the Saints and gentiles had
come to entertain of each other gave the Mississippi river outlaw bands an excellent chance
to make use of Nauvoo as a place of refuge.
By professing Mormon views, they at once,
when charged with misdemeanors or crimes,
were able to raise in the minds of the Saints
a presumption that they were being maligned
and persecuted; hence they were given pro·
tection. But be the explanation what it may,
the offenses were committed and 'the Mormons held responsible for them. So common
a practice had horse stealing become that the

river crossing between Nauvoo and Montrose
was widely known as the "thieves' ferry." It
had even a more sinister reputation: tales
were told of how the Danites, mounted on
fleet horses, would seize men against whom
death had been decreed by their organization,
strap them behind them, be ferried to the
centre of the stream, and there cut out the
entrails of their victims and sink their bodies
in the water. People on both sides of the
Mississippi lived in constant dread, hardly
daring to unbar their doors after nightfall.

In May, 1845, a German family in Lee
county, Iowa, (the county in which is the village of Montrose) was murdered in a manner
exceptionally brutal. The murderers, the
Hodge brothers, were tracked to Nauvoo by
Edward Bonney, and discovered to be living in a remote part of the town. Their
house was surrounded, they were captured,
and, after a trial and conviction, hanged
Bonney was a remarkable character. He kept
a livery stable in Montrose, traveled much on
the river, and knew many of the members of
the outlaw bands. He has been charged with
having been an outlaw himself, but upon no
satisfactory evidence. On the contrary, he
was the means of bringing to justice some of
the most noted desperadoes of the river coun-

try. During the trial of the Hodges great
efforts were made by one of their family to
enlist the interest of Brigham Young in their
behalf, but without result. On another occasion, it is said, an attempt was made in advance by the outlaws to gain the countenance
of Brigham for a criminal project. It was
proposed (so the story goes) by a certain influential Saint of Nauvoo quietly to rob the
chest of a merchant of that town. But the
merchant chanced also to be a Saint. Now,
while Saint number one had no conscientious
scruples against robbery in general, he had
qualms as to the propriety of one Saint robbing another. He therefore sought guidance
from the head of the church. What Brigham's council on this delicate question was
is not known; but when he who sought it
would have carried into effect his original de-
sign, he found Saint number two, gun in
hand, serenely awaiting him.

One of the most celebrated cases of murder attributed to the Mormons was that of
Colonel George Davenport. Colonel Davenport was by birth an Englishman, but, coming
to America, had served this country as a soldier in the war of 1812. He had seen many
adventures both by land and water, and in
Indian times had been a highly esteemed

friend of the old chief Black Hawk.   He now
(1845) was living in a substantial, and, for
the times, elegant mansion on the island of
Rock Island in the Mississippi river, one hundred and twenty miles above Nauvoo.   About
his dwelling towered lofty old oaks ; while
before it, along the margin of a beautiful
greensward, hastened the great stream.   On
the fourth of July, 1845, Colonel Davenport
was sitting in his parlor reading.   His family
were away at a picnic gathering.   Hearing a
slight noise at the rear of the house, he
stepped into the hall to investigate its cause.
Here he was confronted by three men.   One
of the three discharged a pistol at him, the
ball taking effect in his thigh.   He was then
seized, thrown down, bound with strips of
hickory bark, and blindfolded.   Next he was
dragged by his collar and long gray hair up
the broad stairway of his mansion to an upper
room containing a closet in which, in an iron
safe, were his money and valuables.   This safe
the robbers forced him to open.   After securing its contents, chiefly money, they placed
their victim, now weak from loss of blood, on
a bed there was in the room, and demanded
more money.   The Colonel pointed to a
drawer in his dressing table.   The robbers
opened a wrong one by mistake, and, think-

ing they had been deceived, choked their victim till he fainted. This they did twice, reviving him each time by forcing water into his mouth and by dashing it in his face. On his fainting a third time, they fled. Colonel Davenport died from the effect of his wounds on the day following the robbery. To-day, many years after this tragedy and after the Federal Government has purchased Rock Island and made it the site of a great arsenal, the mansion of Colonel Davenport stands solitary and abandoned on the banks of the Mississippi. For a long time the floor of the hall, the steps of the stair-case, and the floor of the room in which the Colonel died, all deeply blood-stained, were shown to travelers. The plastering from the walls and ceiling has now so fallen upon and covered both steps and floors that any traces of blood, if they exist, are hidden from sight. But to continue: The perpetrators of this robbery and murder were ferreted out by Bonney, after some detective work of which the pursuers of Jean Valjean would not have been ashamed, and, with one exception, brought to trial. One of them—Birch—turned state's evidence and made a confession. In this confession, among other things, he said: "The first council for arranging the robbery

of Colonel Davenport was held in Joseph
Smith's old council chamber in Nauvoo."

The effect of occurrences such as have just
been described, and of statements like this one
by Birch, upon the already prejudiced and
excited minds of the anti-Mormons or gentiles,
can well be imagined. On the 1st of October,
1845, a convention of delegates from nine of
the counties adjacent to Hancock county (the
one in which Nauvoo is situated) assembled
at Carthage and passed a resolution that "it
is now too late to attempt a settlement of the
present difficulties upon any other basis than
that of the removal of the Mormons from the
State." On the same day a written promise
that the Mormons would leave the state, as
fast as they could sell their property and
make other necessary arrangements, was
signed by Brigham Young and put in the
hands of a committee appointed by Governor
Ford to confer with the Mormon leaders.
Among the members of this committee was
Stephen A. Douglas. Preparations for departure by the Mormons were rapidly pushed
forward. On November 15th, the *Times and
Seasons* made announcement that fifteen or
twenty thousand persons were preparing for
exodus in the coming spring. It also announced that the number of families repre-

sented in this aggregate of persons was thirty-
two hundred and eighty-five, and that for
their transportation there were fifteen hundred
and eight wagons on hand and eighteen hundred and ninety-two in process of manufac-
ture. The concluding words of the announcement (aimed at the gentiles) were : " O!
Generation of Vipers!"   On January 20, 1846,
a circular to the Saints was issued by the
High Council.   It stated that early in March
a company of pioneers would be sent West to
find some fertile valley near the Rocky mountains where crops could be planted and cabins
built for the sustenance and protection of the
whole body of the Mormon people until a
place of permanent abiding should be determined upon.   The circular stated further,
that should trouble arise with any foreign
power over the Oregon question, the Mormons, despite their wrongs which they keenly
felt, would at least render the American government services as great as those on a certain occasion rendered by a conscientious
Quaker to the crew of a merchant ship
attacked by pirates.   The pirates were in the
act of boarding when one of their number fell
into the water.   As he was fast ascending the
side of the merchantman, by means of a rope
which was hanging over, he chanced to be

spied by the conscientious Quaker. " Friend," said the Quaker, " if thee wants that piece of rope, I will help thee to it," and severed it with his jack-knife. " Much of our property," continued the circular, " will be left in the hands of competent agents for sale, at a low rate, for teams, for goods, and for cash. The funds arising from the sale of property will be applied to the removal, from time to time, of families ; and it now remains to be proved whether those of our families and friends who are necessarily left behind for a season shall be mobbed and driven away by force." The circular emphatically denied that the Mormons ever had cut out the bowels of any person or fed him to the cat-fish. The programme of departure, as laid down in the circular, was not adhered to as to the time of starting, for the first company of Exiles crossed the Mississippi river on the ice on February 5th. During the month twelve hundred wagons crossed. By the middle of May sixteen thousand persons had passed into Iowa and were filing towards the Missouri at a point where now is the city of Council Bluffs.

But meanwhile work upon the Temple had not been suspended. Its exterior for some time had been finished, but within much still remained to be done. As early as October 5,

1845, the windows were in, also temporary floors, seats, and pulpits ; and a congregation of some five thousand had been present at an informal service. By the last of January, 1846, the Temple was as nearly completed as it ever became. At either end of the main assembly room, which occupied the first floor, were the pulpits for the four priesthoods, one above another according to rank ; the lowest for the President of the Elders and his two counsellors ; the next for the President of the High Priesthood and his two counsellors ; the third for the President of the Melchisedeck (Aaronic) Priesthood and his two counsellors ; the fourth and highest, for the President of the whole church and his two counsellors. The last pulpit the Mormons held in the profoundest reverence as a representation of Moses' seat into which used to crowd the Scribes and Pharisees. Beneath the main assembly room was the basement and in it the great Baptismal-fount—a tank twenty feet square, supported upon twelve stone oxen, and ascended by a flight of steps. Above the main assembly room was an upper assembly room, and beneath and above this, in the recesses of the structure, were some small office rooms. There was also an attic story containing a suite of apartments for the use of the

President in the ordinances of washings, annointings, and prayer. Of these different rooms none were wholly finished except perhaps the main assembly room. In the second story the floor was not even laid. Surrounding the Temple square a trench had been dug, some six feet wide and deep, which was to have been filled with masonry as a base for a heavy iron fence. The massive walls of the Temple with their two tiers of round windows, and the environing trench which had been excavated, were but confirmatory proof to the gentiles of the sinister purposes of the Mormons. One suspicious gentile thought the Temple impervious to the heaviest artillery; its round windows port holes; and the trench a foundation step in the erection of a massive stone outwork ten feet high. It was hatred by the gentiles that forced the Mormon artisan, as he wrought at his task during the time of the Exodus, (for the Temple must be completed according to the command of the Lord) to place weapons at his side, while watch and ward were kept from the Temple roof.

That the Temple ever was dedicated with any other ceremony than that of a prayer by Brigham Young on the occasion of the meeting in it of the five thousand in October, 1845, there is no cause to believe. But a picturesque story of a later dedication, which has been invented, ought not to be lost.   According to this tale, the Temple was consecrated at high noon under the bright sunshine of May. From the *rivier Des Moines*, from the land of the Sauks and Foxes, and from near the Missouri, the elders of the church returned to Nauvoo in disguise. Once within the sacred enclosure of the Temple, their disguises quickly were thrown aside and they stood forth in all the splendor of sacerdotal vestments.   The great apartments glowed with the typical emblems of sun, moon, and stars.   The ceremonies were protracted through the night and until the dawning of the next day.   Then the robes were laid aside, the decorations removed, and the company separated as mysteriously as it had come.   The foundation which exists for this tale (and for what tale does not some foundation exist ?) is, according to Joseph Smith, Jr., the fact that, during the Exodus, secret revels were held in the Temple of such a sort as would have brought the blush of shame even to those who in ancient times made the House of God at Jerusalem a den of thieves.   As already has been stated, some sixteen thousand Mormons had crossed the Mississippi river into Iowa by the middle of May, 1845. The remainder continued to leave as fast as they could sell

their effects and buy teams and wagons.   But
the impatience of the gentiles was not to be
restrained.   Under the guise of a sheriff's posse
to enforce the execution of a writ, a battalion
of some six or eight hundred men mustered
in the latter days of August, and, early in
September, took up its march for Nauvoo.
This move was not unexpected by the Mormons, and on September 9th, their sentries
on the roof of the Temple descried the
advancing troops.   On September 12th,
Brockman, the officer commanding the battalion, sent a flag of truce into the town and
demanded its surrender.   The demand was
refused and a skirmish of about an hour's
duration occurred between the invading force
and such of the Mormons as had not yet
crossed the river.   Each side was provided
with a few light pieces of field artillery, and
by those in the hands of the invaders some
damage was done to buildings.   The contest
was brought to an end through the intervention
of a deputation of citizens from Quincy, Ill.,
and, on September 16th, the Mormons signed
an agreement to leave the state or disperse without delay.   They also agreed that in the meanwhile the gentiles should take possession of
the town.   In less than twenty-four hours the
whole Mormon population, now reduced to

about six hundred persons, had gained the Iowa shore. A few, however, were unable to get away, and upon them fell the sore displeasure of the invaders. This was manifested for the most part by the administration of a ducking in the river. Sometimes the ducking was conducted as a baptism ; the victim being first thrown on his back, with the words : "By the holy saints I baptize you ;" then on his face, with the further words : " The commandments must be fulfilled." Limp and dripping he was then sent to the Iowa shore on a flatboat with the injunction ringing in his ears not to come back if he valued his life. Huddled together on the flat ground opposite Nauvoo, poorly sheltered, and with meager food, the Mormons presented a sight truly pitiable. Many were sick ; all were more or less in distress. Nine births took place the first night of the encampment. Moreover, that there might be no lack in the misery of the situation, a thunder storm broke and the rain poured steadily down.

Her people in exile, the city of Joseph was indeed a place of desolation. Thomas L. Kane, of Philadelphia, a brother to Dr. Elisha Kane, the Arctic explorer, chanced to come there a few days after the evacuation, and has left a vivid narrative of what he saw. " I procured a skiff," he writes, "and rowing across the river, landed at the chief wharf of the city. No one met me there. I looked and saw no one. I could hear no one move; though the quiet everywhere was such that I heard the flies buzz and the water ripples break against the shallows of the beach. I walked through the solitary streets. The town lay as in a dream, under some deadening spell of loneliness, from which I almost feared to wake it." . . . . "I went into empty workshops and smithies. The spinner's wheel was idle; the carpenter had gone from his workbench. Fresh bark was in the tanner's vat; and the fresh chopped light wood stood piled against the baker's oven. The smith's forge was cold; but his coal heap and ladling pool and crooked water horn were all there as if he had just gone off for a holiday."

But what concerning the sixteen thousand of the Saints, who, months before this, had begun their march over the prairies of Iowa? At their last meeting in council in Nauvoo, Elder George A. Smith[1] is said to have remarked: "If there is no God in Israel, we are a sucked-in set of fellows; but I am going

[1] George A. Smith became in Utah Brigadier-General of the Mormon militia and first counselor to Brigham Young. He it was to whom Young probably sent the orders which caused the Mountain Meadow massacre.

to take my family and cross the river, and the Lord will open the way." When they set out, the weather was inclement and cold. They advanced in the teeth of northwest winds, which swept with great fury across the naked prairies. Around them lay the withered grass, and much of the time only leaden skies were seen above. The fires of the preceding autumn had destroyed the dry wood along the streams, and in the dearth of fuel it was with extreme difficulty that they kept from freezing. Many were afflicted with catarrh and rheumatism. As the spring came on, heavy rains fell, and the black soil of the prairie was converted into bog. Through it waded and floundered men, women, children, oxen, and horses. A mile or two a day was sometimes all that could be accomplished. Then a swollen stream would be encountered, and the whole expedition would be delayed for a fortnight. Deaths were frequent. The burials were infinitely pathetic. From a log, some eight or nine feet long, the bark would be stripped in half cylinders. The body then would be placed between and the whole laid in a shallow trench. After this there would be a prayer, a hymn, a futile attempt permanently to mark the spot where the loved one had been left, and a resolute setting of the face again to the westward. On April 27th, the Mormon hosts reached a point in what is now Decatur county, Iowa, which they named Garden Grove.   Here, at the call of the bugle, all hands assembled, and an organization was effected for the purpose of putting lands in cultivation and thus providing means of subsistence for the further stages of the journey.   Soon hundreds were at work, felling trees, splitting rails, making fences, cutting logs for houses, building bridges, digging wells, and making plows.   A strong detachment was then separated from the main column to occupy the new settlement.   On June 17th, at a point in what is now Union county, Iowa, which the Mormons called Mt. Pisgah, another settlement was made. .A little later and the main column was at the Missouri, on the extreme limit of Iowa Territory, near where now is located the city of Council Bluffs.

While on the march, the Mormons still had continued to be an object of mingled curiosity and fear to the gentiles. Tales concerning them had been freely invented.   One of these was that, when in the Sauk and Fox country, a party of the Saints, clad in spangled crimson robes and headed by an elder in black velvet and silver, had been seen teach-

ing a Jewish pow-wow to the medicine men.
Another tale was that the Mormons were going about among the Iowas in short frocks of
buffalo robe, in imitation of John the Baptist,
teaching baptism and the kingdom of Heaven.
Still another tale was that an elder, with long
white beard, and who spoke the Indian language, because he had the gift of tongues, was
distributing powder and whiskey to the Yankton Sioux.   Finally it was darkly whispered
that the Saints were in the pay of the British
government, and were carrying to the Pottawattomies scarlet uniforms and a battery of
twelve brass field pieces.

The hills on the Iowa shore of the Missouri,
where the Mormons stopped, are bold and
high, and from Indian times have been
called the council bluffs.   On these hills, and
on the level land at their base, were pitched
the white tents and drawn up the white-topped
wagons of the exiles.   It was full summer.
Herd boys tended sheep, cows, and oxen
on the slopes.   At the river margin, women
washed the soiled garments of their families.
Smoke rose high into the air from a thousand
camp fires.   The scene was varied and filled
with animation.   To make it even more so,
the Pottawattomie Indians sent a deputation,
under their distinguished Chief Pied Riche,

to confer with the Mormons, and a council was held. Each party represented either had suffered, or believed it had suffered, wrong at the hands of the government, and this created a strong bond of sympathy. Pied Riche himself was a savage of some pretensions towards higher things. He spoke French with ease. His daughter, Mademoiselle Fanny, played on the guitar, and showed her sense of the requirements of hospitality by entertaining some of the maidens among the Mormons at a coffee supper.

Soon after the Mormons reached the Missouri, they were waited upon by Captain Allen, of the First U. S. Dragoons, for the purpose of enlisting from their numbers several companies for the Mexican war. "You shall have a battalion at once," Brigham Young is reported to have said, "even if it be a class of our elders." So the companies were raised, and preparations made for the march against Mexico. A farewell ball was given. It was held under a great arbor or bower made from poles and branches. The Mormon belles, as described by Stenhouse, were sweet and clean in white 'stockings, bright petticoats, starched collars and chemisettes. The first dance was a double cotillion of elders and their partners. This was followed by French fours, copenhagen jigs, and virginia reels. The music was from violins, horns, sleigh-bells and tambourines. When the frolic was over, the military recruits were called forward and blessed by the authorities of the church, and on the next day were fairly off for the war.

The main body of the Mormons (as already has been stated) remained in the camp on the river bluffs till the spring of 1847. They then resumed their momentous journey westward into the wilderness. And as they went, they sang:

"The time of winter now is o'er,
    There's verdure on the plain;
We leave our sheltering roofs once more,
    And to our tents again.

Chorus.

O, camp of Israel, onward move;
    O, Jacob, rise and sing;
Ye saints, the world's salvation prove;
    All hail to Zion's King!"

THE FIRST MEETING WITH THE
DAHKOTAHS

THE FIRST MEETING WITH THE DAHKOTAHS.

" Very fierce are the Dahkotahs."—Longfellow.

FOR an unknown period of time before the year 1600, the Dahkotah, or as they are now generally called, the Sioux, Nation of Indians, ranged that part of the continent of North America extending from the Rocky mountains to Lake Superior and the Mississippi river, and from what are now the British Provinces southward to about the parallel of forty-two degrees north latitude. They were wise in council and fierce in war. In these respects they resembled the Iroquois. Indeed they were called by the Jesuit missionaries sent among them the Iroquois of the West. The *Relation* of 1671–2 says: " These quarters of the North [West] have their Iroquois as well as those of the South [East] ; who make themselves dreaded by all their neighbors. Our Ouatouacs [Ottawas], and Hurons had up to the present time kept up a kind of peace with them ; but affairs having become embroiled, and some murders even having been committed on both sides, our savages had reason to apprehend that the storm would burst upon them, and judged that it was safer for them to leave the place." Thomas G. Anderson, who figured on the side of the British at the taking of Fort Shelby, Prairie du Chien, in 1813, and who had been an old trapper among the Sioux, thus wrote in his journal concerning these Indians as late as the beginning of the present century. "I must do the Sioux the justice to say that on the whole they are the most cleanly, have the best regulations as a tribe, . . . are the swiftest pedestrians, best bow and arrow men, the most enormous eaters at their feasts, yet can abstain longer without food, than any of the [other] numerous tribes I have met."

The name Dahkotah means "friendly" or confederated tribes, and is the only name by which this people are known to themselves. Their name Sioux is a modification of the final syllables of the Ojibway word Nadowai-siwug. Nadowaisiwug literally means "like unto the adders," and is the name by which the Iroquois always have been known to the Ojibways. It was the early French mission-aries and traders who first abbreviated it to *siwug* and then modified *siwug* to *sioug* and *sioux.* The elimination by the French of the sound for which the English letter *w* stands was most natural, for this sound is not represented in the French alphabet. Charlevoix writes in his admirable history: "The name Scioux that we give to these Indians is entirely of our making, or rather it is but the last two syllables of the name Nadouessioux, as many nations call them."

The origin of the Dahkotahs, like that of the other nations of Indians in North America, is unknown. They perhaps came into Minnesota from the region north of Lake Superior where they had had conflicts with the Esquimaux. The first attempt to classify them was made by Le Sueur in 1700. He discriminated them into Scioux of the East and Scioux of the West. Later attempts have resulted in classifying them in three divisions. The first division is the Issati, Isanyati, or Issanti, Sioux — those who ranged to the Eastward of the Mississippi river. The name Issanti seems to have been derived from Isantamade or Knife Lake, one of the Mille Lacs, Minnesota, near which this branch once lived. The second grand division of the Dahkotahs is the Ihanktonwan, (pronounced E-hawnk-twawn) or Yankton ; this name means "Village at the End." The Yanktons lived west

of the Issanti, ranging to the Missouri river.
The third division is the Tee-twaun or Tintonwan. This name means "Village in the
prairie." The Tintonwans ranged from the
Missouri river to the Rocky mountains, and
were the fiercest and most warlike of their
nation.

At different times from 1615 to 1634, the
Chevalier, Samuel de Champlain, Governor of
New France, had heard it said that four hundred leagues to the West of Quebec there
dwelt a people that formerly had lived near a
distant sea, and who on that account were
called the Tribe of the Men of the Sea. It
was told, moreover, that this Tribe of the Sea
held intercourse with a people living still farther
West who reached them by crossing a vast
expanse of water in large canoes made of
wood, instead of bark, and who, because of
their shaved heads, their beardless chins, and
their strange costumes, might perhaps be the
Tartars or Chinese. Stimulated by a wish to
know if Tartary or China could be reached
merely by crossing the American Continent,
Champlain employed Jean Nicolet, a clerk
and interpreter of the Company of the Hundred Associates, to undertake a journey of
discovery. Nicolet set out on the first of
July, 1634. He at length reached the Hurons

who lived near the entrance to Lake Superior.
His journey thence is best described in the
words of the Jesuit *Relation* of 1643. "He
embarked from the territory of the Hurons
with seven savages ; . . . . . when they arrived there, [the country of the Men of the
Sea], they drove two sticks into the ground
and hung presents upon them to prevent the
people from taking them for enemies and
murdering them. At a distance of two days
journey from this tribe, he [had] sent one of
his savages to carry them the news of peace
which was well received, especially when they
heard it was a European who brought the
message. They dispatched several young
men to go to meet the manitou, that is, the
wonderful man ; they come, they escort him,
they carry all his baggage. He was clothed
in a large garment of China damask strewn
with flowers and birds of various colors. As
soon as he came in sight, all the women and
children fled, seeing a man carry thunder in
both hands. They called thus the two pistols
he was holding. The news of his coming
spread immediately to the surrounding places
—and four or five thousand men assembled.
Each of the chiefs gave him a banquet, and at
one of them at least one hundred and twenty
beavers were served."

This country of the Men of the Sea into which Nicolet had come, was the country of the Winnebago Indians which lay south of Green Bay in what is now the State of Wisconsin. The people to the west of the Men of the Sea, who were supposed by Nicolet to be Asiatics, and for whose edification he had donned his robe of yellow damask, he neither met nor saw. They were the Dahkotahs—the denizens of the wilderness beyond the Mississippi.

The first men of European extraction to meet any of the Dahkotah nation, and to leave a record of the fact, were Pierre d'Esprit, Sieur Radisson and his brother-in-law, Médard Chouart, Sieur Groseilliers. These men had formed a partnership "to travel and see countreys," as Radisson expressed it. In this occupation they spent the years from 1658 to 1685. Radisson kept a journal of their travels from 1658 to 1664. In 1665 he and his companion were in London courting the favor of King Charles II. As one means of securing it, Radisson copied out this journal and took pains to have the copy put into the King's hands. Through this channel Radisson's narrative finally came into the possession of the diarist and Secretary of the Admiralty, Samuel Pepys. In

1703, Pepys' manuscripts were scattered and Radisson's narrative was obtained by the collector Richard Rawlinson. From him it drifted into the Bodleian library where it now is. But to resume. In 1659, the Sieurs Radisson and Groseilliers visited the town of the Mascoutins, situated on Fox river, thirty-seven miles from Green Bay. The Mascoutins "told us," says Radisson, " of a nation called Nadoneceronon wch is very strong wth whom they weare in warres." These Nadoneceronons were in fact the Dahkotahs—the people spoken of in 1689 by Perrot as Nadouesioux, and in 1767 by Carver as Naudawises; in other words, the Sioux.

Our travelers, however, did not come in actual contact with the Dahkotahs or Sioux till 1662. In that year they crossed the Mississippi and ascended into the Mille Lacs region of what is now the State of Minnesota. While here, writes Radisson, " there came 2 men from a strange country, who had a dogg. These men were Nadoneseronons. They were so much respected that nobody durst not offend them, being that we were upon their land wth their leave." Some two months later than this the Dahkotahs sent a deputation of eight of their young men to visit Radisson and his party and convey to them assurances of friendship. The ambassadors brought with them a present of skins of the buffalo and beaver, and in these the travelers at once arrayed themselves. The Indians then literally fell upon the necks of their new found friends and wept, until, in the words of Radisson, " we weare wetted by their tears." They next produced the peace pipe, no ordinary tobacco bowl, Radisson wishes it understood, for he describes it as only brought forth " when there is occasion for heaven and earth." And indeed the pipe seems to have been of good workmanship. The bowl was of red pipe stone, and as large as a man's fist. The stem was five feet long and an inch in diameter. Attached to the stem, near the bowl, was the tail of an eagle, spread like a fan, and painted in different colors. Along the stem were fastened the feathers of ducks and of birds of gay plumage. After an interval of silence, Radisson and his companion prepared some squibs which they threw into the fire about which the party were seated. The explosions that ensued caused the Sioux to spring up and flee in terror. "We followed them," says Radisson, " to reassure them of their faintings. We visited them in their apartments where they received us all trembling for

feare, believing realy by the same meanes
that we weare the Devils of the Earth."

About five days after these occurrences
thirty young Dahkotah braves arrived armed
with bows and arrows. The arrows were
pointed with bits of stags' horn. The dress
of these Indains was scant and their bodies
were highly colored with paint. On the next
day came a large band of Dahkotahs. " They
arrived," says Radisson, " with an incredible
pomp. This made me think of ye Intrance
yt ye Polanders did in Paris, saving that they
had not so many Jewells, but instead of these
they had so many feathers." First among
them were young warriors armed with the
bow and arrow and buckler. The buckler
was carried on the shoulder and upon it were
drawn representations of the sun, the moon
and of wild beasts. The faces of the warriors
were daubed with paint. Their hair had been
made to stand erect through the application
to it of a paste made of grease and red earth,
after which the ends had been singed off until
they were even. On the crown of the head
was the usual scalp lock, to the extremity of
which depended a few bits of turquoise. Some
wore attached to the head, with fiendish contrivance, the horns of the buffalo ; others the
paws of the bear. The ears of many were

pierced with five large holes from which hung
coppear trinkets shaped like the half moon
or the star. All wore highly ornamented
leggins and moccasins. Besides the bow and
arrow and buckler, they carried knives eighteen inches long, ingeniously shaped stone
hatchets, and wooden clubs. Close on the
heels of the young men followed "the elders."
They were clad from head to foot in buffalo
robes and bore themselves with imperturba-
ble gravity. Besides the calumet each of
"the elders" carried a medicine bag in which,
according to Radisson, "all ye world was
enclosed." They had not painted their faces,
but they wore the same head dress as the
young men. Bringing up the rear of the procession came the women laden like mules.
Indeed, almost hidden from sight, were they,
under their enormous burdens, the weight of
which, our narrator naively hopes, "was not
equivolent to its bignesse." In less than half
an hour the women had unslung their bundles,
taken from them the tent skins, and erected
the teepes.

A council then convened at which the Dahkotahs, after much talk complimentary to the
travelers and to the French nation, made
a present to the former of buffalo and beaver
skins. They did this by way of courting an

alliance with the French, their thought being, according to Radisson, "that the true means to gett the victory was to have a thunder," (fire arms) with which the French were well supplied. After the council a feast was announced. Four beautiful maids, carrying bear skins, preceded the travelers to the place where the feast had been prepared. One of Radisson's party then indulged in some singing, after which, says Radisson, "we began our teeth to worke." The meal consisted, among other things, of wild rice. At its end the travelers made gifts to their entertainers of "hatchets," knives, awles, needles, "looking glasses made of tine," little bells, ivory combs, and a pot of vermilion. A special gift of necklaces and bracelets was made to the Indian maidens who had served at the dinner. "This last gift," says Radisson, " was in generall for all ye women to love us and give us to eat when we should come to their cottages." The Indians expressed their gratification at this munificence by shouts of Ho! Ho! Ho!

The travelers next paid a visit to the nation of the Christinos who dwelt a seven days journey to the northward of the Mille Lacs. They then returned to the Bœuf band of the Dahkotahs, with whom they had held the council above described. This time, however, they went to the principal village of the Bœufs which consisted of permanent, rectangular lodges like those which the Sacs and Foxes afterwards built near the mouth of the Rock river in what is now the State of Illinois. This village, Radisson thinks, contained a population of seven thousand souls. The summering grounds of these Dahkotahs were further South—probably near where is now located the city of Dubuque in the state of Iowa.

After six weeks spent at the village of the Bœufs, Radisson and Groseilliers, taking a final and friendly leave of the Dahkotahs, set out in the direction of the Sault Ste. Marie.

THE TRAGEDY AT MINNEWAUKON

THE TRAGEDY AT MINNEWAUKON.

AMONG the hills and prairies of Northwestern Iowa are the three lakes, East Okobogi, West Okobogi, and Minnewaukon. Minnewaukon or Spirit Water is the largest of the three. It is circular in shape, and covers an area of twelve square miles. To the east of it the country is bare and rolling; to the west are low bluffs dotted with groves. In the thought of the Indian it was the abode of spirits; he regarded it with superstitious awe, and is said never but once to have profaned its surface with canoe and paddle. On this one occasion an Indian maiden, captured in a far land, had been rescued by her lover, and with him had taken flight across the lake. In blind rage her captors cast away prudence and launched their canoes in pursuit. Midway in the passage a storm arose; the outraged genii of the place appealed to the gods of the wind and thunder, and the daring and impious band were overwhelmed. East Okobogi (okobogi means place of rest) begins at the foot of Minnewaukon, from which it is narrowly separated, and extends southeastwardly for about six miles. It is slightly below the level of Minnewaukon, and its general appearance is that of a broad and tranquil river. West Okobogi is the most beautiful lake in Iowa. Its waters are as transparent as those of Garda; they have been sounded to a depth of perhaps two hundred feet; objects beneath them have been distinguished at a depth of fifty feet. Its shores are broken into bold capes and headlands, and its beaches are broad and hard. It is of a curved or horseshoe shape, and lies directly south of East Okobogi. Indeed it is separated from its gentle sister on the north only by a slender strait. Its direction is first southwestward for nearly five miles; then, in a graceful curve, an equal distance to the northward. It was called by the Indians Minnetonka or great water, to distinguish it from its sister lake.

To-day these three lakes, like nearly all such bodies of water in America, are the resort of large numbers of tourists. Forty years ago they were solitary and almost unknown. The groves of oak and elm along their shores were twined and festooned with the woodbine, the wild grape vine, and the ivy. Herds of shy deer assembled at their edge to drink. On the point of some long tongue of land the elk bent down his head to the water, while his perfect reflection looked up at him from beneath. In the autumn, after the leaves on the trees had turned to yellow and red, flocks of wild ducks and geese, flocks countless in number, that at times darkened the air with their plumage, came steadily on from the north till the lakes lay spread below; then suddenly wheeled and descended into them with a mighty splash and with many a squawk and flutter.

At this early time in the history of the Northwest, Minnewaukon and its companion lakes were yet within the borders of the great territory dominated by the Dahkotah or Sioux nation of Indians. In general the limits of this territory were the river St. Peter's on the east, the Rocky Mountains on the west, the Canadian possessions on the north, and an uncertain line on the south near the parallel of forty-five degrees north latitude. Excepting only the Iroquois, the Dahkotahs have been the most remarkable people of purely Indian characteristics upon our continent. Their name Dahkotah (confederated bands) is that given to them by themselves; their name Sioux is from Nadesioux, the word used to designate them by the early French traders and explorers. Nadesioux, however, is not a proper noun; it is merely a Gallicized form of the Ojibway word Nadowaisiwug (adders or enemies), and was employed by the Ojibways as descriptive of the Iroquois as well as of the Dahkotahs.

The first meeting of the Dahkotah Indians by white men took place at a spot not so remote from this lake region of Iowa. In 1662 the French travelers, Radisson and Groseilliers, held a council with a large company of the Dahkotahs near the Mille Lacs, in what is now the State of Minnesota.[1] They were even then a famous and dreaded nation. Says Radisson, in his quaint, Gallic way: "They were so much respected that nobody durst not offend them." In subsequent years their tribal organization was studied. They were found to be separated into three great divisions: the Issanti, (of which the principal band was the Meddewakantonwan) the Yanktons, and the Tintonwans. The Issanti extended to the east of the Mississippi river. It was by them that Father Hennepin was made a prisoner in 1680, and by them that the death of the good father was for a time seriously meditated for the prize of his priestly vestments. The Yanktons and the Tintonwans lived west of the Mississippi.

[1] See the paper in this volume entitled, The First Meeting with the Dahkotahs.

The Tintonwans were the fiercest and also the most westerly of the Dahkotahs. They dwelt on the plains. Their name, indeed, indicates their place of habitation ; it means dwellers in the prairie. The number of the Dahkotahs—taking them in all their branches—originally was large, and continued to be so down to recent years. It was placed by the earliest French writers at forty thousand. In 1763 Lieutenant James Gorrell, the British officer in command at Detroit, placed it at thirty thousand. In 1852 Rev. Stephen R. Riggs, a missionary among the Dahkotahs, thought it to be twenty-five thousand. In 1837 the Issanti division ceded all its lands east of the Mississippi to the United States, and retired to the region of the St. Peter's river in Minnesota. Besides the Meddewakantonwan band of the Issanti, there was also the Wakpekute. This band was in constant war with the Sacs and Foxes of Iowa until the removal of the latter from Iowa territory in the year 1845. There were two chiefs of the Wakpekute : Wamdisapa or Black Eagle and Tasagi. Wamdisapa and his immediate followers were savages of such unusual ferocity and ardor that they could not dwell at peace even with their own band. They therefore separated from it and went west to the lands on the Vermillion river. So complete was this separation that in 1851, when the Issanti tribe ceded the territory owned by them in Minnesota, Wamdisapa's contingent was not deemed a part of the Wakpekute band and was not asked to join in the treaty.

Among the followers of Wamdisapa was a brave by the name of Sidominaduta. On Wamdisapa's death this brave became chief of the band. He was holding this position at the time of the settlement of the country about Fort Dodge in Iowa, and with his band was often in the vicinity of the Fort. He was always regarded with distrust and fear by the settlers. One winter's day in 1854 he was found dead upon the prairie. An aged crone who was living in his family, his squaw and two of his children were found dead in his lodge. They all had been killed by a trader named Henry Lott, who immediately afterwards had burned his dwelling and fled the state. According to the story told by those of the chief's family who survived, (a boy twelve, and a girl ten, years old) Lott and his son one morning had met the chief near his lodge and urged him to go in quest of some elk which they said they had seen feeding in the bottom lands. Thereupon the chief had taken his rifle, mounted a pony and ridden off. Lott and his son had stealthily followed him and shot him. At night on the same day the settler and his son, disguised as Indians, had come to Sidominaduta's lodge and killed his entire family, save themselves; they had escaped by hiding. In spite of the evil reputation of the leading victim of this tragedy, no cause for Lott's act ever could be found, and a wish by the Indians to avenge it no doubt had something to do with subsequent events.

Sidominaduta being dead, his brother, Inkpaduta, or Scarlet Point, who also had been a follower of Wamdisapa, became chief. Inkpaduta fully sustained the reputation for ferocity borne by both his predecessors in office. He had killed, it is said, Wamdisapa's co-chief, Tasagi, because of Tasagi's comparative mildness of disposition, and to open the way for the elevation of his own family to the chieftainship. He was six feet tall, of strong frame, his face ugly and deeply pitted by small-pox. No picturesque sight could he have been as he lounged in his tepee surrounded by dirty, screeching, fighting children, and squaws of an exterior and deportment as little prepossessing; the whole party —if in the game country—greedily despatching a meal of uncooked bison's liver; and, if on short commons, still more greedily devouring half-singed skunk meat or putrescent fish. He must have appeared positively terrifying and revolting when decked for war; his face daubed with black streaks, eagles' feathers in his hair, and malignant light lurking in his eyes.

In 1856, some six or seven families, embracing forty persons, built cabins for themselves along Minnewaukon and the Okobogi lakes. At a point in Minnesota (now the town of Jackson) eighteen miles north from the lakes, a half dozen families also had built cabins. Forty miles to the south of the lakes were a few other settlers. To the east, near where Emmetsburg now stands, were five or six more families. There were also some scattered farmsteads to the southwest along the Little Sioux river. All were about equally new and raw, and about equally exposed upon the frontier. The winter of 1856–7, in Minnesota and Iowa especially, was memorable for severity and for long duration. It began early in December and continued far into April. Snow fell to a depth of three feet on level ground. ·High winds prevailed, and whenever the ground or objects offered a sufficient obstruction, immense drifts accumulated. Moreover, it was fiercely cold; ice formed with

almost instantaneous quickness.   In the well
settled parts of Iowa roads were blockaded
business brought to a stop, and great suffering
entailed.   How life fared with the pioneers of
the lake country, most of us can with difficulty
imagine.   Their houses were of logs, entrance
to which was barred only by rude, wooden
doors, hung on wooden hinges and fastened
by wooden latch pieces.   Many of them had
no floors.   In others prairie grass had been
spread over the ground and secured in place by
a covering of rag carpet.   Heat was obtained
from the stove on which the scant meals of the
family were cooked.   There were no supplies,
other than game, except as they were brought
from points distant nearly a hundred miles.
It was at night, more especially, that a sharp
sense of the solitude and isolation of their
position was forced upon these people.   The
hard lakes gleamed in the clear light of the
moon.   All else of nature was snow hidden ;
mystic, beautiful, yet inexpressibly desolate
and waste.   Wolves cried, and the snapping
and cracking of the frost-pervaded forest
raised in the minds of the startled hearer
visions none the less appalling that they were
ill-defined.   Or it was a night (and there
were many such at the lakes) on which a
blizzard, a visitation literally from the land

of the Dahkotahs, was sweeping down upon
the settlement.   The north wind—the veri-
table Kabibonokka of Indian legend—

" Howled and hurried southward."

Before it were driven the fine snow crystals,
pitiless upon the cheek as powdered glass.
They sifted through the chinks of the cabins,
accumulating in little piles upon the flooring,
upon the bed clothes and upon the faces of
the sleeping children.   On such a night there
was absolutely no safety without.   A strong
man would have perished twenty paces from
his own door.

At last, after many weeks marked by
weather such as has just been described, there
came a milder and less tempestuous season.
It was March.   Indians were encamped at
different points about the lakes and on the
Des Moines river.   There were some Yanktons and there was Inkpaduta's band.   Around
Minnewaukon were twenty tepees; near
Springfield (Jackson) Minnesota were fifteen
or twenty more.   There also were four or
five at Big Island Grove, a place some six
miles southeast from where now is the town
of Estherville.   This last mentioned camp
was presided over by the chief Ishtabahah or
Sleepy-Eye.   It was the opinion of Major
William Williams, who led the relief expedi-

tion—to be described later on—that this mar-
shalling of Indians betokened a plan on their
part to devastate and depopulate northwestern
Iowa. Be that as it may, I am now to relate
the events which actually transpired.

On the morning of March 8th, the family
of Rowland Gardner — a settler living on the
south shore of Lake West Okobogi — rose
early so that Gardner himself might gain
time for the journey to Fort Dodge on
which he was to start that day. Rowland
Gardner's family comprised his wife, a
daughter of thirteen, a son of about six, a
married daughter, her husband, her little
son, and her infant. While breakfast was
in progress, an Indian entered and asked
for food. He was at once given a seat at the
table with the family. Soon other Indians
came until the cabin was filled with fifteen
braves together with their squaws and pa-
pooses. They were no other than Inkpaduta
and his band. All were liberally provided
with such food as the family had in store and
ate greedily until satisfied. They then became insolent: demanded ammunition and
many things besides. One of them snatched
a box of gun caps from the hand of Gardner;
another tried to seize from the wall a horn of
powder, but in this was foiled by Gardner's

son-in-law, Luce.   The Indian who had been foiled then drew up his rifle, apparently to kill Luce, but did not discharge the weapon. At this juncture two of the neighboring set-tlers, Dr. Isaac Harriot and Bertell Snyder, called at the Gardner cabin to leave letters to be taken to Fort Dodge.   Gardner told them he could not leave his family that day as the Indians evidently were in an ugly mood. Harriot and Snyder made light of this opin-ion, did some trading with Inkpaduta's party, and then went to their own cabin on the peninsula between the Lakes East and West Okobogi.   At noon the Indians left the Gard-ner house and strolled off toward that of another settler, James Mattock, which stood near the cabin of Harriot and Snyder.   A con-sultation was then held by the inmates of the Gardner house.   It was decided to warn the other settlers.   At about two o'clock Luce, and a man by the name of Clarke, who seems temporarily to have been staying with the Gardners, set forth on this errand.   At about three o'clock the report of rifles discharged in rapid succession reached the Gardners from the direction of the Mattock cabin.   After some two hours of wearing anxiety and sus-pense, Gardner unbarred his door and went out to reconnoiter the ground.   He hastily returned, saying that nine Indians were approaching the house and that the inmates were all doomed to die. He wished, however, to barricade the door and make a determined fight. This his wife and married daughter persuaded him not to do, but still further to trust to the policy of conciliation. It was now five o'clock. The day had been one of exceptionally fine weather. The sun had risen in a cloudless sky and the sky was yet clear and blue as he neared his setting. A huge ball of flame he sank slowly beneath the horizon lighting up the lakes and the whitened prairie with a crimson glow. The nine Indians who had been approaching now entered the cabin. One of them roughly demanded meal. Gardner turned to get it, and was instantly shot through the heart. The women, excepting Abigal Gardner, the daughter of thirteen, were then beaten over the head by the Indians with the butts of their rifles, dragged into the cabin dooryard, and scalped. What next occurred is best told in Abigal Gardner's own words. She says: "During these awful scenes I was seated in a chair, holding my sister's baby in my arms; her little boy on one side, and my little brother on the other, clinging to me in terror. They seized the children, tearing them from me one by one, while they reached their little arms to me, crying piteously for protection that ·I was powerless to give. Heedless of their cries, they dragged them out of doors and beat them to death with sticks of stovewood."

Abigal Gardner was made a captive by the Indians and taken to their camp which had been erected about the Mattock cabin. Here she was met by a sight no less terrible than that which she had just beheld. It was night, but the woods were illuminated, both by the camp fires of the Indians, and by the flames of the burning cabin. Scattered over the ground were the mutilated remains of eleven persons, men, women, and children. Within the burning cabin were two more victims, not yet dead, but rending the air with shrieks of agony as the flames devoured them. There were some slight evidences of resistance on the part of the settlers. Dr. Harriot lay with a broken rifle grasped in his hand. Rifles were lying near the bodies of Mattock and Snyder. Their work of death finished for the present, the savages celebrated it by the war-dance. "Near the ghastly corpses and over the blood-stained snow;" says Abigal Gardner, "with blackened faces and fierce uncouth gestures; and with wild screams and yells, they circled round and round, keeping time to the dullest, dreariest sound of drum and rattle, until complete exhaustion compelled them to desist."

The next day the cabins belonging to the other settlers about the lakes were visited by Inkpaduta and his party, and the inmates either shot or brained with clubs. The wives of three of the settlers, Noble, Thatcher, and Marble, were taken captive as had been the daughter of Rowland Gardner. The Indians then made ready to quit the country of the three lakes and Iowa. Before doing so, however, they peeled a section of bark from a large tree that stood near the Marble cabin, on the west shore of Minnewaukon, and on the white surface thus exposed left in picture writing a record of their deeds. The number of persons killed by them (thirty-two in all) was indicated with entire accuracy by rude sketches of human figures transfixed with arrows. There was also a sketch of the Mattock cabin in flames.

The fact of this massacre in the lake region of Iowa was discovered on March 9th by Morris Markham, a man who had been living at the house of Noble and Thatcher, but who was absent when the attack by the Indians was made. He fled with the news to

Springfield, Minnesota. He also communicated it to two settlers upon the Des Moines who carried it to Fort Dodge. There at first it was deemed an idle tale. But on March 22d, three men well known in Fort Dodge returned from a prospecting trip to the shores of Minnewaukon and the Okobogis and confirmed what already had been heard.

An expedition, composed of nearly one hundred men from Webster City and Fort Dodge, was at once organized at the latter place to go to the lakes. Supplies for the journey were carried in wagons drawn by teams of oxen and horses. Among the men was Cyrus C. Carpenter afterwards governor of Iowa. The party was under the command of Major William Williams of Fort Dodge, a man of much experience with the Indians. The start was made on March 25th. Great difficulty was found in marching. The weather for a time had been mild, and the depressions in the prairie were covered by a mass of snow and water, three or four feet deep. In order to break a road for the wagons, the men were formed in a solid column and marched forward several rods. They were then faced about and marched back over the same course. Next the wagons were unhitched from the teams and driven ahead by the united strength of the command. When stopped by an accumulation of snow in front, shovels were resorted to and the obstruction cleared away for another advance. The horses and oxen proved to be much harder to drive forward than had the wagons. They sank to their bellies in the snow and slush and became utterly helpless. They were only rescued by hard pushing, pulling, and lifting. On the 28th, the party reached a place called Shippey's, on Cylinder Creek. On the 29th, they reached the Irish colony near where now is the town of Emmetsburg. On the 30th, they came to Big Island Grove on Mud, now High, lake.

Here they discovered evidences that their of approach had been watched by the band Ishtabahah or Sleepy-Eye. On Big Island, which stands in the middle of the lake, grew a tall cedar tree, and in its branches, forty feet from the ground, the Indians had built a platform. From this elevation it was possible to see a distance of twenty miles in all directions. Fires were yet smouldering where the Indians had made their camp; several fish were lying on the ice of the lake near holes which but recently had been cut; a half-finished canoe was upon the lake shore. On the 31st, the command of Major Williams

met a party of twenty fugitives from Minnesota, and learned from them that, a few
days after the massacre in Iowa, Inkpaduta's
band, together with a number of Yanktons,
had made an attack on Springfield. Several
settlers had been killed, but they had escaped
and were fleeing to Fort Dodge for safety.
This party consisted of three men and seven-
teen women and children. Some of them
had been painfully wounded in the attack,
and all were suffering from cold, hunger, and
exhaustion. They were sent to the Irish settlement by Major Williams, and the advance
continued. On April 1st, the command
reached Granger's Point, near where Estherville now stands, and also near the Minnesota
line. During the preparations for encampment, a mounted soldier of the regular army
was seen approaching. From him it was
learned that troops from Fort Ridgley, Minnesota, were then at Springfield, and that
Inkpaduta's band and their allies, the Yankton band, had escaped.

This news was highly unwelcome and dis-
heartening to the volunteers, as they had
hoped to reach the lakes in time to inflict
punishment upon the perpetrators of the
massacre. But further advance would have
been useless, and on the morning of April

2d, the entire command, save a squad of twenty-six men which was sent out to inter the dead bodies at the lakes, faced about and began their homeward march.   On April 4th, Major Williams with the main party reached the banks of Cylinder Creek.   The weather was warm and had melted the snow so rapidly that the creek was out of its banks and the prairie inundated as far as the eye could see. The men were weary; their clothes torn and wet; their boots soaked.   Moreover they were without food and the materials for a fire. While in this exposed place and in this reduced condition, the weather suddenly changed.   At about four o'clock in the afternoon, the wind swept into the north and began blowing a gale.   It grew intensely cold.   The air was filled with fine snow and sleet.   In short, a blizzard — that terror of the plains in the Northwest—had broken and was fast swinging into full career.   Nothing remained for the command but to go into camp for the night where they were, bleak and inhospitable though the spot.   Accordingly they removed the canvas top to the one wagon which they still had with them, and spread it, together with some tent cloth, across the wagon body.   They then staked the sides of this covering, as best they were able, to the frozen earth. Snow was banked up against the improvised shelter on all sides save the south, where an opening had been left for ingress. Opposite this opening they stationed the horses. The party then made with their blankets a bed in common, and crept into it. At intervals it became necessary to renew the embankment of snow which the terrible wind had scattered. Here, without fire, without food, in frozen garments, and with the thermometer thirty-four degrees below zero, the command remained huddled together from Saturday night until Monday morning. On that morning, April 6th, the storm subsided. The waters of Cylinder Creek were found to be hard ice, and on this a crossing was made. Writing in 1887, Ex-Governor Cyrus C. Carpenter said: "Since that experience on Cylinder Creek, I have marched with armies engaged in actual war. During three and one half years of service the army with which I was connected marched from Cairo to Chattanooga; from Chattanooga to Atlanta; from Atlanta to the Sea; from the Sea, through the Carolinas, to Richmond. These campaigns were made under southern suns and in the cold rains and not infrequent snow storms of southern winters. They were sometimes continued for three or

four days and nights in succession, with only
an occasional halt to give weary, foot-sore
soldiers a chance to boil a cup of coffee.
But I never, in these weary years, experienced
a conflict with the elements that could be
compared with that of the two nights and
one day that I passed on the banks of Cylinder Creek."

It was near this creek that the detachment
which had gone to the lakes to bury the dead
there, rejoined the command. They had
suffered even more grievously than their
companions. On reaching the place of the
massacre, they had dug shallow trenches in
the hard soil and deposited within them the
stiff and mangled bodies of the settlers. They
had then started back. They had waded
sloughs waist deep ; had tramped to and fro
all the night of the blizzard in order to keep
from succumbing to stupor and perishing ;
had terribly frozen their feet. Some of
them, finding their feet useless, had crept
weary distances on their hands and knees.
Some had become delirious and bled at the
mouth. Two of their number had become
separated from the others and lost. In
fact they had died of cold and exhaustion
upon the prairie where their bones, identified
as theirs by the rusty rifle barrels beside

them, were not found until eleven years afterwards.

With the arrival of the survivors of this detachment in the camp of Major Williams, the
expedition, as an organized affair, came to an
end. The men separated and found their
way home in various sad plights and by different ways.

In the meanwhile Abigal Gardner and her
three sister captives were trudging painfully
towards the Northwest as slaves and menials
in the train of Inkpaduta. Aside from the
captives and the Indian women and children,
the individuals comprised in this train were
Makpeahotoman, or Roaring Cloud, son of
Inkpaduta; Makpiopeta, or Fire Cloud, also
son of Inkpaduta; Tawachehawakon, or His
Mysterious Father; Bahata, or Old Man;
Kechoman, or Putting on as he Walks; Kah-
odat, or Ratling, son-in-law of Inkpaduta;
Fetoatonka, or Big Face; Tatelidashinksha-
mani, or He who makes a crooked Wind as
he Walks; Tachonchegahota, or His Great
Gun; Husan, or One Leg, and perhaps two
or three others. One of the braves was
wounded and was borne in a litter. He had
sustained his wound at the hands of Dr. Harriot, and was the only member of Inkpaduta's
band injured at the lakes. Through the day-

time it was the lot of the captives to carry on their backs enormous burdens. They were not provided with snow-shoes, as were the Indians, and consequently made but slow and toilsome progress. At evening they deposited their loads, cut fire-wood, and aided in erecting the tepees. These exactions came hardest upon the wife of Thatcher. When captured her nursing child had been torn from her breast and killed. In her susceptible condition exposure gave her cold, and she was attacked by fever. An abscess formed in one of her breasts. One of her legs swelled to twice its natural size, turned black, and burst some of the blood vessels. Despite all this she was granted no respite from labor. She marched under a heavy pack, as did the other women, and with them struggled through snow drifts and the cold water (the latter at times waist deep) of creeks and sloughs. One day, soon after the attack on Springfield, the band halted for rest near a stream bordered by clumps of willow. While there the Indians descried a company of the Fort Ridgley regulars far away on the prairie. In feverish excitement the former hid their squaws and plunder among the willows, loaded their rifles with ball, and set a guard over the captives, while one of the band climbed into a tall tree

near by to see if the troops would advance or
retire.   The order to those guarding the captives was short and explicit: to shoot them
on the instant if the troops advanced.   The
troops did not advance, as the Indians were
not discovered by them, and were thought to
be a journey of two or three days' in the
lead.

The country through which the Indians
were taking their way was entirely wild, and
hence fitted to exert upon the mind that peculiar effect of mingled charm and awe which
only wild places can.   In it was the famed
pipe-stone quarry whence, from time imme-
morial, the Dahkotahs had obtained the beautiful material for their calumets : the material
from which had been made the pipe smoked
by Radisson and Groseilliers on the occasion
of their first meeting with the Dahkotahs in
1662—a pipe the size and appearance of which
had much impressed Radisson.   The quarry
is situated in an alluvial flat which is walled
in on all sides by bluffs and cliffs.   At one
spot in this flat is a huge boulder supported
upon a table-rock of smooth and glistening
surface.   On both the boulder and its supporting rock have been graved the figures of
lizards, snakes, otters, Indian gods, rabbits
with cloven feet, muskrats with human feet,

and other strange things. According to the legend, these figures were traced by the hand of Gitche Manito, the mighty. A party of Yankton and Tintonwan Dahkotahs one sultry day had assembled at the quarry to dig pipe-stone. Suddenly there came from the sky heavy peals of thunder and zig zag flashes of lightning. The Indians ran to their lodges in terror of what they thought to be an approaching tempest. But on peering forth from their shelter, instead of a tempest they beheld a tall pillar of smoke resting upon the boulder. For a time it swayed to and fro, then gradually assumed the shape of a giant. With one long arm the figure pointed toward heaven and with the other to the rock at its feet. Again there were peals of thunder and vivid flashes of lightning which drove the Indians into the depths of their lodges. Again they looked forth, but this time saw nothing unusual; the giant had disappeared from the boulder, and only twilight held possession of the valley. On visiting the boulder the next morning, however, the Dahkotahs found both it and the table-rock beneath it covered with the mysterious emblems above described. According to another version of the legend, (the one made use of by Longfellow), Gitche Manito, the mighty, after impressing the figures on the rocks,

"Smoked the calumet, the peace-pipe,
As a signal to the nations;"

*   *   *   *   *   *   *   *

And in silence all the warriors
Broke the red stone of the quarry,
Smoothed and formed it into peace-pipes,
Broke the long reeds by the river,
Decked them with their brightest feathers."

Familiar with these ancient legends of their nation, Inkpaduta's band stopped at the pipe-stone quarry and spent a day in the agreeable occupation of studying the pictured rocks and of shaping pipe bowls.

At the end of six weeks from the date of the massacre, the Indians reached the Big Sioux river at about where now stands the town of Flandrau, South Dakota. The scenery was striking. "From the summit of the bluffs," writes Abigal Gardner, could be seen "thousands of acres of richest vale and undulating prairie," through which, "winding along like a monstrous serpent, was the river, its banks fringed with maple, oak, and elm." While crossing this river on a natural bridge of uprooted trees and brush, one of the captives, the wife of Thatcher, was pushed into the stream by a young brave, and her attempts to gain the shore thwarted by him and others

of the band, who forced her back into the
current with long poles. As she was drifting
away she was shot. From this time on wan-
dering bands of Yanktons were occasionally
met, and to them the members of Inkpaduta's
band would narrate with savage glee the
deeds which they had done in the country of
Minnewaukon and the Okobogi lakes. The
wife of Marble, after much bargaining, was
purchased by two Indians belonging to one
of these bands and brought to Charles E.
Flandrau, agent of the United States government for the Sioux Indians at the agency on
the Yellow Medicine river, in Minnesota.
The fate of Noble's wife was like that of Mrs.
Thatcher. She was killed by her captors.
She had resisted Inkpaduta's son, Roaring
Cloud, in some excessive demand and thereupon was immediately brained by him with a
club.

It was now early June. "The prairie,"
says Abigal Gardner, "as boundless as the
ocean, was decked and beautified with a carpet of various shades of green, luxuriant
grass. The trees along the streams put forth
their leaves which quivered on the stems.
The birds, arrayed in their gayest plumage,
flitted among the trees and sang their sweetest
songs, while the air was redolent of the per-

234 THE TRAGEDY AT MINNEWAUKON.

fume of countless flowers." "We crossed one prairie so vast and so perfectly devoid of timber that for days not even a hazel-brush or a sprout large enough for a riding-whip could be found. The sensation produced by being thus lost, as it were, on the boundless prairie was really oppressive. Exhausted as I was, and preoccupied as my mind was by other things, I still could not ignore the novelty of the situation. As we attained the more elevated points the scene was really sublime. Look in any direction, and the grassy plain was bounded only by the horizon. Then we would journey on for miles till we reached another elevation, and the same limitless expanse of grass lay around us. This was repeated day after day, till it seemed as if we were in another world. I almost despaired of ever seeing a tree again. The only things to be seen, except grass, were wild fowl, birds, buffalo, and antelope. The supply of buffalo seemed almost as limitless as the grass. This was their own realm, and they showed no inclination to surrender it, not even to the Sioux."

At one point in this prairie, (the scene perchance of some hard battle of long ago) was found an Indian place of the dead. Scaffolds of poles, eight or nine feet high, fifteen feet

long, and six feet wide, had been erected and
on them in compact rows had been laid a
great number of bodies. Only the bones of
these now were left ; in some instances cast
to the ground by the winds. The Indians
paused at this place of the dead and closely
examined its relics, especially the skulls.
These they took in their hands, bent and
chattered over them; then carefully replaced
them upon the ground or scaffolds.

Not long after the death of Noble's wife,
Inkpaduta's party arrived at the James river.
Here, on the spot where is now the town of Old
Ashton, South Dakotah, was a Yankton encampment comprising one hundred and
ninety lodges. These Indians evidently had
never before seen a Caucasian. They stared
at Abigal Gardner in complete amazement,
commenting on the light color of her hair
and eyes. Still more astonished were they
when her white arms were exposed to them
and the fact communicated that, when first a
captive, her face (since reddened by paint
and exposure) was as white as were now her
arms. The rifle was as yet an unfamiliar
weapon to this large band. Only the club,
spear, and the bow and arrow were visible
about their persons or in their tepees.

At this time Abigal Gardner had given up

all hope of being rescued. At each remove
her captors were leading her deeper into the
wilderness. A life in a Dahkotah lodge or
as a beast of burden to a Dahkotah warrior
upon the trail seemed to be all that the future
held in store. But, after the recovery of Mrs.
Marble, the Indian agent, Flandrau, and
Governor Medary, of Minnesota Territory,
had diligently set about effecting the ransom
of the remaining captive; and while yet in the
Yankton camp she was purchased by Indian
emissaries from the Agency on the Yellow
Medicine. During the negotiations prelim-
inary to the purchase, Miss Gardner's captors
indulged themselves in a piece of fiendish
pleasantry. They told her that she was to be
put to death. The manner of her death was
differently described by different braves.
Some by appropriate gestures signified to her
that she was to be cut in small bits, beginning with her fingers and toes and ending
with her heart ; others that she was to be
drowned ; still others that she was to be
burned at the stake. But at length a bargain
with her deliverers was struck and she was
given into their hands. The price paid for
her was two horses, twelve blankets, two kegs
of powder, twenty pounds of tobacco, thirty-
two yards of blue squaw cloth, thirty-seven

and a half yards of calico and ribbon, and some other small articles. Her restoration to liberty and civilization was now not long delayed. Before her final leave taking, however, Matowaken, the great chief of the Dahkotahs, made her a gift. It was made to her, she was told, in recognition of the fortitude of spirit which she had displayed in captivity, and was, at least from the point of view of a Dahkotah, of inestimable value. It consisted of an Indian head-dress elaborately and skilfully made. The foundation of it was a close fitting cap of finely dressed buckskin. Around this, so as to form a crest, were set thirty-six of the largest feathers of the war eagle. These feathers were painted black at the tips, then pink and black alternately in broad bands to the base of the crest. Below the base of the crest, the cap was covered with the white fur of the weasel, the tails of the animal hanging as pendants.

That Inkpaduta himself, or that any one of his band, except Roaring Cloud, ever suffered punishment for his bloody deeds in Iowa is doubtful in the extreme. For a time the annuities were withheld from the whole Dahkotah nation, the threat being that they would only be renewed upon the delivery of Inkpaduta and his followers to the government for trial. But this action so incensed the Indians, and put in such jeopardy the lives of settlers among them, that it was discontinued upon a representation made to the authorities by the chief Little Crow that he had pursued Inkpaduta's band and killed three of his braves. It was Little Crow who in 1862 directed the memorable massacre of settlers along the St. Peter's river in Minnesota. The probability of his statement that he had wreaked vengeance upon Inkpaduta in behalf of the whites is certainly somewhat shaken in view of his own subsequent career. According to every indication Inkpaduta, so far from being to Little Crow an object of abhorrence, was his model. Roaring Cloud was killed. He ventured back to the Yellow Medicine to woo, it is said, some Indian maiden. But his presence was revealed by an enemy, and a detachment of soldiers from Fort Ridgley hemmed in the spot where he was. He fought his pursuers, but soon fell pierced by many balls.

In December, 1883, Abigal Gardner, for the first time since 1858, again stood within the walls of the cabin built by Rowland Gardner, her father. She says: " All the years that had intervened seemed obliterated, and everything appeared the same as in the time long gone. The snow-covered ground, the oak trees with the seared leaves clinging to their boughs, all were the same as on that eventful night. As the shadows darkened, I could almost see the dusky forms of the savages file up to the door-way, rifles in hand ; crowd into the house ; shoot my father when his back was turned ; drive my mother and sister out of doors ; kill them with the butts of their guns ; tear the children from my arms and beat them to death with clubs. . . . . . Having retired to rest, the swarthy creatures seemed all about me murdering, plundering. . . . . . Again when the morning broke and I heard the prattle of the children of the household, it seemed as though they were the very same whose merry voices had been so suddenly changed to dying groans. I could hardly realize that twenty-seven years lay between that dreadful night and this morning's waking."